# WIRTH

DIRTY ACES MC

LANE HART

D.B. WEST

# COPYRIGHT

This book is a work of fiction. The characters, incidents, and dialogue were created from the authors' imagination and are not to be construed as real. Any resemblance to actual people or events is coincidental.

The authors acknowledge the copyrighted and trademarked status of various products within this work of fiction.

© 2021 Editor's Choice Publishing

All Rights Reserved.

Only Amazon has permission from the publisher to sell and distribute this title.

This book or any portion thereof may not be reproduced or used in any manner whatsoever without the express written permission of the publisher except for the use of brief quotations in a book review.

Editor's Choice Publishing

P.O. Box 10024

Greensboro, NC 27404

Edited by Angela Snyder
Cover by Melissa Gill Designs

**WARNING: THIS BOOK IS NOT SUITABLE FOR ANYONE UNDER 18. IT CONTAINS STRONG LANGUAGE, VIOLENCE, AND GRAPHIC SEX SCENES.**

# SYNOPSIS

Trouble is coming for the Dirty Aces MC when they least expect it.

After a patch-over party turns into a near fatal shootout that injures several members, the Dirty Aces MC is left reeling.

Wirth feels especially guilty since he wasn't at the bar when his brothers needed him the most. Instead, he had left with a beautiful, mysterious woman, making some of the new members question his loyalty to the club.

Needing to clear his own name, Wirth intends to find out who the rat is within the MC. Suspicious of the new girl, Maeve, he decides to try and get closer to her to determine where her true loyalties lie.

Once he finds out Maeve's secret, Wirth's own loyalties may be shaken to the core.

# PROLOGUE

*Maeve Donovan*

"I'm begging you, Cormac, let my brother go!" I've tried reasoning with Rian to leave town with me, but he refuses. He'll never budge on his own. I need someone else to help me free him from the chains of the ridiculous sense of duty my father laid on his shoulders so that we can both have a normal life for once.

Smirking behind his lowball glass of amber liquid, the cliché redheaded Irish asshole in a black perfectly tailored suit says, "Come on now, Maeve. You act as if I have Rian tied up in the basement like a captive. He knows he can leave the cause whenever the hell he wants."

"But he won't leave, and you know that!" I shout at him. "He thinks he has to fulfill some…some stupid promise he made to our father, to follow in his footsteps. He won't ever walk away from you or this chaos unless you throw him out!"

"Rian's eighteen now – a grown ass man, who is loyal and strong with one hell of a good aim. He can make his own decisions, sweetheart. He no longer needs his big sis to try to protect him."

I grit my teeth at his condescending tone. Men are all the same – self-centered assholes who only care about themselves.

"And you don't need Rian to protect you either!" I point out to him. "Just because he brags about hitting the bullseye of a practice target doesn't mean anything. He'll probably end up killing himself before he shoots anyone else!" I huff.

"You don't give the boy enough credit. I wouldn't put him on my detail if I didn't think he had what it takes to back up his cockiness." Cormac chuckles before sipping his whiskey with a grin. I don't miss the irony of him calling Rian a 'boy'. That's what he still is, despite his age.

My brother, the stubborn hothead that he is, insists on staying with Cormac's crew, playing the role of one of his bodyguards. Rian says it's the best way for him to learn how to lead so that one day he can take his place, which is just fucking ridiculous. Cormac can't teach him anything other than how to increase his alcohol tolerance while sleeping with every woman he meets. My brother doesn't need Cormac to show him either of those things. Our father did the exact same thing from the time we were born until the day he died by taking a bullet in his back while fucking some slut in a hotel room. No one saw his killer before he got away. Rian swears he'll find out who it was one day. I would much prefer for him to work on solving that mystery rather than being one of Cormac's henchman.

"Please, Cormac," I plead with him again. I know I'm grasping at straws when I say, "Do you really want to be the man who ends the Donovan line?"

Finally, his smile falters and his skin turns even paler than usual as he quietly considers that scenario while sipping his drink.

Our people may be wanton alcoholics, but they're also superstitious and suckers for tradition. For over a hundred years, a Donovan was the head of the Irish mafia in the United States. It's not a family history that I'm proud of, but it's one that lasted an entire century – that is until my father was murdered last year. His men all voted for Cormac to lead until Rian was old enough to stand on his own.

On his eighteenth birthday, Rian could've stepped into the role, but so far, he hasn't. For some unknown reason, he's thankfully hesitating. Which means there's still time for me to get him free and clear of being the fourth Donovan to also die for the mafia's cause.

"Fine. What you're asking isn't easy, but...I may be able to figure out a way to push Rian out..."

"You will?" I say in surprise.

He holds up his palm. "*After* the new arrivals in the city are handled. If Rian leaves, I could lose the support of other...nostalgic men who may decide to go with him. And with competition coming to town – the cause won't stand a chance of surviving without every last man protecting it."

"How long will it take to get rid of the new guys?" I ask.

Cormac shrugs a shoulder casually under his suit jacket. "I don't want to underestimate our new foe. It could take a year, maybe more. Quick or drawn out, either way, we're looking at a bloody war."

Fuck. War is *exactly* what I'm trying to avoid! What good will our deal be if Rian ends up dead before I get him out of Cormac's grasp?

"Unless..." Cormac drawls.

"Unless what?" I ask.

His green, up-to-no-good, eyes assess me from the top of my long, straight, dirty blonde hair to the toes of my sneakers.

"You're a sexy girl, Maeve."

"And?" I scoff, crossing my arms under my chest indignantly. Men have told me the same thing for years. It's not a compliment, but basically them saying I'm only good for one thing. Besides, there is no way I would sleep with Cormac.

"*And* if you were to use your beauty and sex appeal to charm our new enemies, you could be our little Trojan horse, speeding things along from the inside. So, tell me, how far are you willing to go to save your brother?"

"As far as I have to go," I assure him. That's the truth. While I may only be six years older than Rian, I've been more of a mother to him than a sister. I enjoyed taking care of him, protecting him while we were growing up. If I hadn't, who would have? Certainly not our father who only had children to make an heir for the family business.

He didn't love either of our mothers, and they obviously didn't care for us if they were willing to hand over their babies to him rather than stick around.

If I had been a boy, I probably would've been an only child, so I'm glad I wasn't. For eighteen years, Rian has been all that I have in this world, so I'll do whatever I need to do to keep him safe.

# CHAPTER ONE

*Wirth Wright*

I'm running late to the patch-over party in Wilmington on purpose. I took my damn sweet time disassembling a Porsche that someone brought to the shop this morning for some quick cash. Socializing has never been my strong suit. I prefer spending time with cars and motorcycles in the garage. Vehicles are easy to get along with compared to people – women especially. I always know what to expect when I'm under the hood. Cars have never revved me up and then left me high and dry. Unlike pussy, I can always fit inside of a car, even the tiny ones if I push the seat back as far as it goes. Automobiles are accommodating while most females are not, no matter how much time I spend…aligning their gears beforehand.

So fine, I'm cranky and horny as hell! That's because I haven't had a good fuck in months. Months! But what else is new? Most men would think being well endowed is a blessing, but for me it's a curse that dates back to high school. There I tried for four years to lose my virginity, getting close no less than six times. I always ended up sending the girls running.

I can count on one hand how many times I've actually finished inside of a woman in all of my twenty-five years. The number of mouths to finish me has only been maybe twice that amount, and usually they have me come on their tits or face, rarely down their throat.

Tonight, I'm sure there will be plenty of pussy for the other men, but none that can handle me. So, once I get to the bar, I'll be on my own for the rest of the night. All but one of my brothers in the Dirty Aces MC have settled down for good, so they'll be cozied up with their old ladies. And while Fiasco may always be good for a few laughs, he's no doubt already balls deep in the first woman he met at the Knights of Wrath's party. Unlike me, Fiasco doesn't need the jaws of life to wedge his dick into a tight cunt.

I probably should've just stayed at the shop working rather than make the half-hour drive. It's not like I even voted to let these guys wear our patch.

A year or so ago, all six of us voted against patching the Knights of Wrath in because they were deep in the black tar market and their ancient president was a humongous dick.

Over the last few months, though, crazy old Bobby G. did a little too much of his own heroin and croaked, putting Hunt in charge.

The Dirty Aces voted again recently, and a majority agreed to patch the Knights over if, and only if, they were willing to set up shop in Wilmington to help out with our speed and gambling enterprises there. We didn't think they would actually take us up on the offer; but apparently, they all wanted a fresh start in a new city. Which leads us to the patching over tonight.

The sun set hours ago, but that's fine with me. I enjoy riding west through the cool summer nights on my new Yamaha without the sun blinding me. The pavement below my tires and the trees on either side of the highway are nothing but inky blurs as I open the throttle as far as it will go until I have to slow up to take my exit.

It's there at the top of the dark ramp that I see a car pulled over onto the grass – a little white car that glows under the light of the moon. It only takes a second to determine it's a Honda Accord.

My first thought is that, if it's still there tomorrow, I'll send our tow truck out to haul it back. Honda parts are a big seller and one of the easiest cars to move through the chop shop.

Then, thanks to my headlight, I spot movement along the passenger side – the top of a golden head before it disappears out of sight.

Curious, I ride off the shoulder and circle around in the grass. My headlight then lands on a blonde woman in a black dress kneeling beside the back tire. She turns her pretty young face to squint at me for only a second before she goes back to work, tugging roughly on the lug wrench.

I'm sure there are plenty who can do the same out in the world; but in all my life, I've never actually witnessed a woman on her knees with a tool in her hand trying to change her own tire. It's the hottest thing I've ever fucking seen.

Do they make female mechanic porn? If so, then I've been missing out, because nothing is as sexy as the sight before me even if she's totally fucking clueless.

I put the kickstand down on my bike and turn off the engine. Before I can even get my helmet off, she mutters without turning around, "I've got it! I don't need any help!"

Huh.

"You sure about that, doll?" I call back as I swing my leg over to stand up. I place my helmet on the seat and then walk over to her, pulling out my phone as I go to light her up again. I consider taking a picture but first things first. "You jack that wheel up right there and your car's going to roll right down the hill."

"The parking brake is on."

I make a quick assessment to ensure none of her body parts are behind the wheel before letting her proceed to jack the car up, mostly because the sight is making me hard but mostly because I'm realizing she's not going to toss the tools down and just let me do it for her.

It starts slow, just a few inches before the car really starts moving.

"Shit!" the woman exclaims as she jumps up. She starts toward the trunk like she's going to stop the momentum of three thousand pounds of steel rolling downhill.

I do act now, snatching her with my arm around her waist and holding her backside to the front of my body as the car begins to pick up speed.

"What are you doing? Put me down!" she exclaims as she starts to kick and squirm, drowning me in her strawberry and vanilla scented hair. Her car really picks up momentum as it rolls down the hill, the flat tire she had been loosening flying off just before the little Honda slams into a row of trees.

"Congratulations, doll," I say next to her ear. "You found the only hill on the east coast, the worst place to stop and change a tire."

The fight goes out of her body, but her words are still sharp. "I could've stopped it if you had let me!"

"I'm sure that when the tires ran your body over it would've slowed down significantly, but it still would've ultimately ended up in the trees."

"You're an asshole!" She pushes at my arm around her waist, so I let her go. It's not easy to restrain her with my brick of a phone still in my hand.

"I'm trying to help you and probably just saved your life!"

Spinning around, she yells, "You could've just told me!"

"Like you would've listened, Miss I've Got It and Don't Need Any Help." I shine my phone on her to get a better look at her face but only get a glimpse for a second before she covers it with her palms.

"Sorry." The word is muffled like she hates saying it. "I'm running late and was just in a hurry. Now I'm fucked."

"You're not fucked," I assure her. "I can give you a ride wherever you need to go tonight. Tomorrow, I'll have a tow truck take your car to my shop and fix it up for you."

"Really?" she says, her voice full of disbelief when she finally lowers her hands.

"Yeah, really."

"What's the catch?"

"The catch?" I repeat in confusion. "There's no catch."

"Yeah, right. There's always a catch when it comes to men like you," she says as she stabs her fingers through the front of her silky straight locks to push it out of her face.

"Men like me?" I echo.

"You're big and buff with the fast bike and patches. I know what those mean. You're all the same."

"You know a lot of bikers?" I say in surprise as a sudden stab of jealousy gets me in the gut. Why do I care what kind of men she runs with? We just fucking met. Still, I don't like it.

"Yeah, I do. In fact, they're going to be pissed that I'm running so late. Their dicks won't suck themselves."

"Wait," I say, holding up my palm because I don't want to imagine her on her knees for some other man. I prefer the image of her on her knees trying to change a tire or her on her knees for me. That fantasy is completely ruined if she gets passed around like a bong that everyone gets to hit. "Don't tell me you're going to the Knights of Wrath patch-over party too."

"Oh. Um, so you know the Knights?" she asks, all stubbornness gone. Now she sounds…nervous, scared even.

"Yeah, I know them. They're about to become the Dirty Aces MC tonight."

"They're patching over?" she says in surprise.

"That's right."

"Tonight?"

"Yes."

She bites down on her bottom lip in thought, making me think of dirty things before she mutters, "I just thought it was a regular party. Patching over means…does that mean more protection?"

"Something like that," I agree with a sigh. "At least we're going to the same place. Makes it easy for me to give you a ride."

She casts a longing look at her car that's half in the forest, half in the grass.

"I'll come and get it tomorrow," I promise her. "Give me your number so I can keep you updated. When it's fixed, I'll bring it to the bar, okay? No strings. No catch."

"Then why would you do it? Why would you help me if you don't want something from me?"

It's obvious by the way she says 'something' that she means sex. And while I would give anything to fuck her, I'm not going to hold car repairs over her head just to get in her panties. Like I could fit even if I wanted to.

"I'm just trying to be a decent human being for once," I assure her. "Now, do you want a ride or not?"

"Guess I don't really have a choice," she replies before rattling off her phone number that I quickly type into my phone. I'm about to ask her name when she starts to walk away. "Hold on. Let me get my purse and make a quick phone call."

She jogs down the hill to her car like she's in a hurry to get away from me. Maybe she's going to call a friend and tell them where her car is and give them the license plate on my bike as a precaution. I can't fault her for that.

Even in the dark of the night I can tell she's a beautiful woman with sexy curves, the kind of body men would kill to see naked.

Suddenly, I can't help but wonder who she's been fucking or sucking off in the Knights – the lucky bastard. These parties are always rowdy, so there's a chance I may get to see for myself. And while I would rather be the man who gets to be with her, I may have to make do with just watching.

# CHAPTER TWO

*Maeve*

The handsome biker mutters something I don't catch when I end my phone call and make my way back up the hill. My hands are shaking with nervousness. What if I just made a huge mistake? It's too late now. There's no point in feeling guilty. I'm just doing what any other sister would do for her little brother. Right?

"Did you hear me?" the man asks when I'm standing next to him again.

"What?"

"I said my name is Wirth." He holds out his big hand for me to shake.

As I take it, sliding my small palm into his, soaking up the warmth of his skin, I ask, "Worth as in 'how much is my wrecked car worth?'"

"Close but with an 'I' instead."

"Wirth."

"Yeah," he replies. "Are you going to tell me your name?"

Shaking the rest of my second thoughts away, I tell him, "Oh, right. I'm Maeve."

"Maeve," he repeats, and I can see the white of his teeth in the dark when he grins. "Nice name."

"You could thank my father, but he's dead."

"Sorry," he replies.

"It's fine," I tell him. It really is. I never loved my father or had an emotional attachment to him. He was just the man who gave me and Rian the basics in life, what we needed to survive.

"So, what do you do at the Knights' bar? You a waitress or something?" he asks as we walk back to his bike. He hands me his helmet from the seat.

"No, I'm a club girl."

"Oh," he mutters with a heavy exhale. "So, which of them are you fucking?"

"Why do you care?" I ask as I lower the helmet over my face.

"Just wondering who is going to be pissed if they see you on the back of my bike."

"Nobody will care."

"That's what you think," he grumbles as he throws a leg over his motorcycle seat.

"They won't. I'm just a piece of ass they all share."

"All of them?" he exclaims.

"All of them," I repeat as I climb up on the back of his bike and grab his waist that's rock hard, not an inch of fat on it. "Sometimes all of them at the same time."

"Oh yeah?" I feel his breath hitch either in arousal or...jealousy. "All of them at the same time?"

Wirth is even bigger up close like this, with his enormous wide shoulders and thick round biceps. And he smells comforting, like leather and...summer. Freshly mowed grass and sunshine. It's an intoxicating combination. And a man as buff and sexy as him has surely had a few threesomes before even though he's acting like having sex with multiple people at the same time is a crazy idea.

"Well, they've all fucked me except for the prospect," I tell him honestly. I thought I had prepared myself for what I would have to do to get close to the Knights, so I went right for Hunt, the president. I can't say I expected him to insist on letting the other four guys have a turn the same night while he watched. It was an initiation, Hunt said; and unless one of the men claimed me, I would always be fair game for them all. Well, except for the prospect. "They let the prospect go down on me, get me good and ready for them, but he doesn't get to come in one of their girls until he patches in."

Wirth is a motionless statue against the front of my body, not even breathing. I can't tell what he's thinking. Has he labeled me a slut? A whore? I've certainly been called worse. Besides, it's true.

"And you like being with...all of them?" he finally asks.

Isn't that a loaded question? The answer is yes and no, but I can't exactly go into the details with a stranger.

"A girl's gotta do what a girl's gotta do, right?" I respond. The past few weeks have been a mixture of mostly pleasure, a little pain, and the total destruction of my dignity. But I'm doing what I have to do to help Rian. If that means a short time of discomfort now to ensure he lives a long life away from the violence, then it will be worth it. Besides, I lost my innocence a long time ago.

Without another word, Wirth cranks his bike and takes off toward the Knights' bar and clubhouse, thankfully ending our discussion.

I'm not proud of the things I've done, but I would do them again in a heartbeat if it means getting me and Rian away from the Irish mafia once and for all. He's the only real family I've ever had. I've protected him his entire life, and one way or another I will get him free of the claws of Cormac.

As soon as we arrive at the Knights' clubhouse, Wirth backs into a spot in the well-lit parking lot that's lined up with bikes, twice as many as usual. I quickly climb off his bike and yank off his helmet, offering it to him as he remains seated.

"Thanks for the ride, I guess."

"You guess?" He turns his face toward me after removing his goggles, then slides his fingers through his black hair to smooth it down the side part. And for the first time I get a good look at his face in the light. He's...beautiful. With full, kissable lips, dark blue eyes, and just a thin black beard outlining his strong jawline, he takes my breath away.

In another life, I wouldn't mind letting him play the role of the white knight coming to my rescue.

But in real life, I know such fantasies are absurd. The only person I can count on is myself. I need to be thinking about my plan for tonight. In an hour, Rian said I need to be as far away from this clubhouse as possible. No one will get hurt; he promised me. Cormac is just planning to send a message – a destructive one to warn the Knights away, send them back to Fayetteville where they came from. Rian and Cormac just thought it would be best if I'm not around in case the Knights try to shoot back when they find bullet holes in their treasured bikes.

"I, ah, I need to get inside," I say when I realize I've been standing here for too long staring at Wirth and wanting things I can't have. I gave up on finding love and romance a long time ago.

"Yeah, see ya," he replies before I turn and reluctantly walk away from him.

## CHAPTER THREE

*Wirth*

"Look what the cat finally dragged in," Malcolm, the president of the Dirty Aces MC, says over the sound of a hard rock song playing from the speakers when I finally stroll into the dimly lit Knights' bar after Maeve came inside, leaving me wanting more of her. No surprise, Malcolm's girl Naomi is on his lap, Silas is making out in the corner with Cora, Devlin is cozying up with Jetta at the bar, and Nash and Lucy are nowhere to be seen. I suppose they are probably still home fucking, or maybe even in the bar bathroom getting it on.

"I'm here. Now how long do we have to stay?" I grumble when I pull out the empty chair at the square table. It doesn't look like Naomi will need her own seat anytime soon.

"How have you been, Wirth?" his girl asks sweetly.

"Good. How about you?"

"Same old," she replies with a big smile. "Malcolm dragged me out of the house tonight and away from Honey. It's a blessing to be away, but I also have a nagging ache to get back to her."

"Time away from the little one will do you good," I reply. "So, what did I miss?" I ask Malcolm.

"The Knights of Wrath are no more," he says proudly, meaning they've already commenced with the patch over that will bring more money and more power to the Dirty Aces. I glance around the room and see several guys donning their brand-new leather cuts with the Ace of Spades skull patches and the same logo hanging from a banner behind the bar. Without a thought, my eyes are also searching for Maeve in the crowded room, although I'm not sure if I want to see some asshole's hand on her ass or tongue down her throat. She's an odd one. Beautiful but…stubborn and independent, which only makes her even sexier. In the parking lot, I finally got to see just how tight her black dress was over her curves, a pair of leather knee high boots making her legs look a mile long and hinting at the inch or so of bare skin peeking out from under her short ass hem.

It's fucked up that my first thought when she mentioned the gang bang by the Knights was that I bet she could take my big dick just fine. Not that I would ever be part of whatever it is that has them sharing women. That's a fistfight waiting to happen, and she ain't worth the trouble. Probably.

"You all right, man? You look a little high-strung tonight," Malcolm remarks.

Leaning closer to him and Naomi, I say, "Did you know these guys pass the club girls around like a joint? They all hit some of their girls the same night!"

"So?" Malcolm grunts. "You scandalized? Offended, even?"

"So, that's pretty fucked up, isn't it?" I ask, looking to Naomi to back me up on this.

"Not much different than taking turns with the same girl on different nights, is it?" Malcolm replies, referring to the women back home that used to go through the Aces like a revolving door.

"Guess not."

"Hmm," Naomi mutters while she glances around. "These younger guys are pretty hot. Much better looking than the old ass Knights."

"Watch it there, honey," Malcolm says when he grips her jaw to turn her face back to him so he can kiss her lips forcefully. "You've got all the cock you can handle right fucking here."

A second later and he's pulling Naomi around so that she's straddling his lap.

"Oh, Jesus Christ," I grumble as I get to my feet to escape the couple. "I need a drink, and you two need a room!"

At the bar, I wedge my hip into the overcrowded row and wave my hand to get the bartender's attention, in desperate need of some alcohol.

He nods in my direction and holds up a finger while filling up someone's glass of beer. I pull out cash from my wallet while I wait, still looking around for Maeve, who I can't seem to find. Where the fuck is she? Off screwing one of the newest Dirty Aces already?

"What can I get you?" the bartender, an older man with greying hair and a beer gut, finally asks when he makes his way to my end of the bar.

"Let me get a bottle of Crown Royal," I tell him, slapping down two twenty-dollar bills.

"A shot of Crown Royal?" he repeats over the noise of chatter and rock music.

"A whole fucking bottle," I tell him since it's going to be a long night. By the looks of things, the original Aces will be too shitfaced or horny to leave here for home tonight, so I'm guessing we'll be here until the sun comes up. Speaking of horny, I still haven't seen Fiasco's crazy ass...

Finally, the bartender brings me what I want. He eyes the front patches on my cut and then pushes the cash back toward me. "Drinks are on the house tonight for the original Aces."

"Thanks," I tell him, twisting off the top and saluting him with the bottle before I take my first burning sip. As the gold liquid slides down my throat, it leaves a path of fire in its wake that makes me curse. I've barely recovered when a hand lands on my shoulder.

Turning toward the body, I find a golden-haired man with glassy eyes standing too close to me, already two sheets to the wind.

"Wirth! Good to see you, buddy. Hate you missed seeing us get our cuts," Hunt, the club's new president, says. "At least you made it in time to celebrate."

"Yeah, man. Congrats and all that," I tell him, clanking my bottle to his glass.

"It's been a long time coming. Glad we finally made it happen," he says with a smile, still riding the high of him getting voted in as president after Bobby died. He wasn't a man many will miss. "Make yourself at home and let me know if there's anything I can get you. You and Fiasco get first dibs on our girls tonight. The rest of your guys passed, saying they brought their own."

"Thanks," I reply before freezing when a sudden thought hits me. "Where the hell is Fiasco?"

"Last I saw him, your boy was getting his dick sucked by Wanda in the alley while feeling up Crystal."

"Oh, well, good for him," I say with a relieved sigh. At least he's not off somewhere banging Maeve. At least not yet.

"Don't worry. There's still plenty of pussy to go around," Hunt tells me with another slap to my shoulder. "All of our old girls made the trip with us, and we've picked up a few new ones in town too."

"Is Maeve one of your new girls?" I blurt out the question, unable to resist. For some reason, I need to know more about her.

"So, you've already met Maeve?" Hunt asks with a grin. "She's something, isn't she? That little nympho is down for anything you fucking want. You name it, she loves it."

My teeth grind together as he talks about her so familiarly when I've not even been able to lay a finger on her. Hell, I want to, but she made it pretty damn clear that the feeling wasn't mutual. "Unlike you, I don't like to share my women or watch her with other assholes," I admit.

Hunt chuckles and shakes his head. "I hear you loud and clear, buddy. It would be a shame to lose her, but say the word, and she's all yours for as long as you want her."

What kind of asshole talks about women like this, as if she belongs to him and he has some kind of right to pimp her out? I find it hard to believe that the stubborn woman I met earlier tonight would put up with such a thing from anyone. So why in the world does she let these fuckers treat her this way? It doesn't make sense. Something doesn't add up with her.

"Speak of the seductress," Hunt says, and I follow his line of sight to the far end of the bar where Maeve is talking to one of the other women, her purse hiked up on her shoulder. Her lips are painted bright red now and her hair is pulled up off her neck, making her somehow look sexier. I try to read those lips of hers to figure out what she's saying – something about needing to go to the store to get more condoms. Yeah, she definitely said condoms, but then I miss the rest of the conversation because I'm thinking about those red lips trying to stretch their way around my cock.

The women are interrupted by a growl when a burly, tattooed man with a long beard comes up behind Maeve and mauls her. His teeth bite into the right side of her neck like some kind of animal while his greedy hands blatantly and possessively cup her tits from behind before sliding lower. When she jerks her head away to the left, it's impossible for me to miss the wince on her face before she breaks his hold to turn to him, offering the man what I have no doubt is a fake as fuck smile. She says something to him, pointing her finger toward the door, but all I hear is his gruff response, "Upstairs, now!" He spins her in the direction toward the stairs and slaps her ass to get her moving. That's when my feet start heading in the exact same direction without a single command from my head to do so.

"Wait a fucking second," I say when I grab the dick's meaty arm. Maeve's got one foot on the first step of the wooden staircase when she pauses to look over her shoulder. Her eyes widen when she sees me.

"Who the fuck are you?" the giant of a man asks, drawing my attention back to him. I may be a little over six feet tall, but this dude is at least six-six. If it comes to blows over Maeve, I'm not sure if I could take him, but that logic doesn't seem to matter to me at the moment. All I know is that I can't and won't let him take her upstairs tonight.

"Titus!" Hunt says in a warning tone when he comes up behind me. "This is Wirth from the original Dirty Aces. I think he's seen something he wants, so you need to step aside."

"You've got to be fucking kidding, prez!" the ogre grumbles loud enough that everyone's conversations come to a halt. I can feel all their eyes on us, everyone watching and listening over the music blaring from the wall speakers.

"There's enough pussy to go around, big man," Hunt assures him.

"But Maeve gives the best head," Titus whines like a toddler not getting his way.

"She does, but she won't be giving it to you tonight, buddy," Hunt replies with a chuckle when he reaches up to grab the back of Titus's thick neck to urge him toward the bar and away from the staircase. "You two have fun," their president says to me as they walk away.

When the two men are gone, everything begins to go back to normal with chatter and laughter filling the small space again.

"What are you doing?" Maeve asks. Her bright green eyes are narrowed in annoyance when she tucks her arms under her tits like she's exasperated with me.

"Did you want to go upstairs with him?" I question her, already knowing the answer. At least I think I do.

In response, Maeve looks away and lowers her arms, dropping some of her indignant act with them to clutch her purse strap instead. Finally, she shrugs and glances down at the delicate watch on her wrist. "I was about to run to the store to pick up a few things. Do you want to come with me?"

Her question catches me off-guard, just like almost everything else out of her mouth. I cannot fucking figure her out. One minute she's pissed at me for trying to help her and another she's inviting me to go shopping with her?

Before I can give her a verbal response, she sighs and says, "Fine. We'll fuck first, but not upstairs. It's a disgusting pigsty." Snatching my hand, she tugs me along behind her toward the door without another word. I'm not sure if I heard her correctly, but I refuse to ask again in case she changes her mind. Before we leave, I do wave my hand in Malcolm's direction. He barely gives a nod in response before his attention goes back to his woman bouncing frantically on his lap.

In fact, while I was at the bar ordering a bottle of whiskey that was quickly forgotten, it looks like the entire place turned into a goddamn orgy with almost everyone coupled up and getting their freak on.

I can't deny that I'm in desperate need of a good fuck. And I can already tell that Maeve is going to give me everything I need and more if she doesn't change her mind again and punch me in the dick first.

## CHAPTER FOUR

*Maeve*

"Where are we going?" Wirth asks as I pull him toward the sidewalk.

"To my apartment."

"Shouldn't we take my bike?" he asks in a hurry, his voice giving away his urgent need. So much for him 'just being nice.' He's like every other man, only acting the role of a good guy to get laid.

"It's only two blocks away. We'll be there in a second," I reply off-handedly before my conscience gives a twinge. He offered to help fix my car, so it would be pretty messed up if I let his ride get damaged tonight. "You know what, let's take your bike," I agree as I abruptly change direction.

There's a moment of silence, and then he's jerking on my hand, pulling me to a stop so that I have to face him. "Are you sure about this? You seem a little…wishy-washy."

He asks the question like it isn't already a forgone conclusion that he's going to get lucky.

I don't have to think about the answer this time. "Yes, I'm sure," I reply, and it's actually the truth.

Not once but twice tonight this man has appeared out of thin air and saved me from bullshit. The first time with my car I was annoyed because I thought I had everything under control on my own and didn't need any help. But the second, well, I'm grateful beyond belief to not only escape Titus, but the bar itself for a little while. Titus is always a selfish lover who thinks he's so high and mighty that he doesn't need to reciprocate orgasms.

Wirth continues to stare at my face, watching me closely under the light of one of the streetlamps before he finally says, "Okay. As long as you know that this isn't a tit for tat."

"It's not?" I ask, disappointed to learn he's not a giver but a taker.

"No. I'll fix your fucking car either way."

"Oh. Right," I mutter when I realize he's referring to me not needing to pay him back for the car. There's still hope for mankind in bed, or womankind, as the case may be. "So you said. No strings attached. I've got it."

"I mean it," he declares.

"I'm sure you do," I huff with a grin because he just won't quit trying to be the good guy. "Now, can we please get moving?"

The last I checked it was nearly eleven. The clock is literally ticking. I thought a trip to the store would be the best plan of escape, but this, being with Wirth, will work out even better.

"Fuck yes," he replies, the desperation in his voice ringing loud and clear.

"That's what I thought."

"You take the helmet," Wirth says, placing it on my head before he straddles his bike, looking sexier than any man has a right to look. "I'll go slow so you can call out directions."

"It's just the apartment complex on the next right, the apartment at the end on the first floor," I explain, climbing up behind him.

"You live alone?" he asks over his shoulder before cranking the engine.

"Yes. Why?"

"A single woman shouldn't live on the first level. That's where thieves break in first," he explains. And oddly enough, the protective spiel is actually working for me, turning me on even more. Probably because I've never had a man worry about my safety, at least no more than rolling on a condom to make sure he doesn't knock me up.

"I can take care of myself," I say defensively. "And I have a younger brother who visits…"

What the fuck is wrong with me? Why did I tell him that? I've made it for nearly six weeks with the Knights without revealing as much information about myself.

"Glad there's someone to look out for you," Wirth says before he finally gets us on the road, taking it slowly. "Huh," he mutters when we come to a stop a second later. "We could've walked."

"Yeah, I know," I agree. "But, ah, it'll be easier to hop on and get to the store after."

I climb off and hang his helmet on the handlebars to start walking toward my door, Wirth right behind me once he turns off his headlight.

"Right," he agrees. "Wouldn't do to run out of condoms."

Spinning around to face him in surprise, I say, "How did you know that's what I was going to get?"

"I read your lips from across the bar," he says, staring at them now in awe like they're the Holy Grail that he's been searching for his entire life.

Goosebumps cause the hair down the length of my arm to go up at the thought of him watching me without me even realizing it. It's a little…stalkerish, sure, but it also makes me feel safe and protected. That's obviously how he saw Titus approaching me and trying to drag me up the stairs before he intervened.

"Relax, Romeo," I say as I wet my lips with my tongue to enjoy the pained, yearning look on his handsome face. Grabbing the front of his belted jeans to pull him closer, I lean up to whisper in his ear, "You're definitely getting your dick sucked tonight."

Before I can pull away, his arm shoots out, reaching around to squeeze my ass cheek low enough that he also grabs the hem of my dress. So, when he presses forward, his fingertips drag through the crack of my ass, making me gasp because he moved so fast and is so, so close to my pussy.

Now, he whispers in my ear, "And you're definitely getting your pussy fucked by my tongue. That's the only way my cock will ever fit inside of you."

I can't figure out how to respond to that as his fingers find my thong and give it a sharp tug to pull it tight against my clit. I'm all out of teasing and jokes to call bullshit on the exaggeration of his size because I can't think about anything but his face between my legs.

The only word I can verbalize at the moment is, "Okay."

"Okay," Wirth agrees, removing his fingers tangled in my thong to slap the shit out of my ass cheek that's no longer covered by my dress. He hits me hard enough to make me jump as my palms fly out to grab his wide shoulders for balance at the same time my thong becomes soaking wet. "Lead the way."

I would if I could, but it seems that this man, this biker who came out of nowhere, has short-circuited my brain with arousal so sudden and strong that my feet and legs can't remember how to walk at the moment.

## CHAPTER FIVE

*Wirth*

I can't figure out if Maeve is having second thoughts after I slap her ass or if she's turned on. She's frozen in place for several silent seconds until a car horn honks in the distance.

Finally, she moves. Her palms slide down my chest and stomach, then her right hand cups my hard cock through my jeans.

"Jesus, you're big," she mutters as her eyes lower to my appendage. "You weren't joking."

"That a problem?" I ask Maeve.

Most men would love hearing women talk about how big their cocks are in awe, but not me. It's usually the precursor to me trying to wedge it inside them and failing either because it won't go or they change their minds and give me a hand-job instead, which is a poor substitute for fucking.

"God, no," she says, squeezing her fingers around me one more time before she lets go to pull on the shirt under my cut. "Let's go."

We're outside of her first-floor apartment a second later. Maeve retrieves a keyring from inside her purse to unlock the door and let us inside.

I only get to look around the tidy, minimalist space with no pictures on the wall before she pushes me down on the comfy microfiber sofa. After that, she's all I can see when she kneels down between my legs, her fingers working diligently to unfasten my belt to get my fly down. I have to shove my open jeans down my thighs a few inches in order to make room for my dick to be freed from my boxer briefs.

"Holy shit," Maeve says quietly, her eyes widening as she wraps both of her small hands around my thick shaft. I start to think she may change her mind about the blowjob when she opens wide and leans forward, her lips stretching as far as they can to cram the width of my crown into her mouth. It may only be an inch or two, but fuck me, it feels amazing when her tongue coats the underside of my flesh.

All too soon she's pulling her mouth off me. But she's not giving up. Maeve runs her tongue around my head before licking stripes up and down the veins of my length, getting me good and slick so she can stroke me with her hands as she takes me into her mouth again. This time my dick goes a little further, all the way to the back of her throat. I could come right then and there, but Maeve obviously doesn't have a gag reflex as she goes even further before pulling off, sucking me hard as she does.

After that, her head begins to bob in a rhythm that grows faster and faster as I watch in complete wonder while she gives me the best blowjob of my entire fucking life.

Fuck my jealousy from earlier. I don't care how many men Maeve's been with or how many she's had at one time. Now I know it was all worth it for her to learn to be a goddamn goddess on her knees for me.

When her green eyes look up at mine while her mouth is full of my cock, seeking my approval, I realize I'm clutching the sofa cushions so tight they may tear. I'm also biting my lip so hard it's probably bleeding to keep myself from moving or making any sound that could cause her to stop.

Now, I can't hold back any longer.

"Oh, fuck, Maeve," I groan, but it comes out like more of a deep, animalistic growl. Seeking more of her mouth, I slouch lower on the sofa as I grab the puff of hair she pulled up on the top of her head. When she takes the hint, letting me thrust a little deeper down her throat, I start to come as I shout out garbled words that don't make any fucking sense, "*MARRY ME TO-FUCKING-MORROW, WOMAN!*"

That's when Maeve gags for the first time in what I think is caused by her laughing before I pull out of her mouth to tug on my cock. As I finish myself off, Maeve leans forward to take my head back into her mouth, applying suction to the crown to pull my seed from me with force. My entire body jerks and shudders with pleasure – more pleasure than I've felt in fucking years.

"Fuck! Oh, fuck!" I groan through the aftershocks thanks to Maeve's vibrating moans that make it sound like she's enjoying herself as much as I am.

That's impossible.

But I do plan to give her as much pleasure as she gave me.

Reaching down, I grab Maeve's waist and pull her up on the sofa.

"Ah! What are you doing?" she asks with a giggle when she's on my lap, resting her hands on my shoulders.

"Stand up," I order her. "Now."

"Right here?" she asks in surprise.

"Right fucking here."

I help her get each of her feet on either side of my thighs and hold her legs to steady her until she grabs onto the back of the sofa behind my head.

When she's steady, I reach under her dress and jerk her thong panties down to her ankles before I dive underneath the hem. My lips find her inner thigh first, giving it a lick and a bite with my teeth before kissing my way over to her pussy lips. With the first swipe of my tongue on her clit, her legs give out and she's practically sitting on my face, which is absolutely fine with me.

∽

*Maeve*

"OH MY GOD. OHMYGOD!" I scream when Wirth's tongue and lips attack my swollen bundle of nerves. Having a man go down on me has always been the one thing that will loosen me up, ever since my first time when I was terrified...

This isn't anything like that night.

And while I've never come on a man's tongue before, either because they didn't know what they were doing or didn't do it long enough, I think I'm already close. Hell, I can barely hold myself up on the back of the sofa as my knees turn to jelly and my body presses down hard on Wirth's mouth. He doesn't seem to mind. He just keeps going faster and faster, even adding one finger that he slips inside of me, then two. Now, oh god, three!

Based on the embarrassing slurping sounds coming from underneath the skirt of my dress, I'm about to get off like this, standing on a stranger's face.

"Yes, yes, yes!" I cry out in encouragement when he starts pumping his three fingers inside me while the tip of his tongue batters my clit until the room starts to spin and goes dark.

"Oh! Oh, fuck! I'm coming! *I'm coming!*" I scream. And without the least bit of self-consciousness, I press my hips down and ride the waves of pleasure on his face and fingers.

*Jesus Christ.*

Orgasms from sex are *never* this good. Now I know what all the fuss about oral is, and what I've been missing.

I'm still floating in the haze of lust when I hear the crinkle of a foil wrapper. Then, Wirth lowers me, arranging me so that I'm sitting on his lap, my knees spread on either side of his thighs. He tugs the top of my dress down to get his mouth on my tits, then lines up his cock with my dripping wet entrance. Since he's not fully hard yet, he eases right inside, getting thicker and harder each second afterward.

The intrusion is only a little uncomfortable at first until my body stretches to accommodate so much of him in such a tight space.

But after that, I'm slick enough that it feels nice to start moving up and down.

"Fuck yeah," Wirth grunts as I hold on to his shoulders, putting us face to face. His dark blue eyes are heavy with arousal when he says, "That's perfect, doll. Don't stop."

"Couldn't…if I…wanted to," I tell him, and he grabs the back of my head to bring my mouth to his. When he lets go, our eyes remained locked on each other, our lips close enough to softly brush on every slow downstroke as I ride him. Both of us are almost awestruck and completely captive to this moment in time.

It's the closest I think I've ever felt to anyone during sex, like it's not just about him trying to get off in a hurry, but he's making sure it's good for me too. Not to mention that if we go any faster, he could possibly tear me apart now that he's rock hard again.

## CHAPTER SIX

*Wirth*

"That's it. Oh yeah, that's so…fucking…good," I tell Maeve through my clenched jaw, letting her control the speed and depth as we fuck. It's all I can do to keep myself in control and not throw her down on her back to pound into her tight pussy like a jackhammer.

I have to admit that slow is good too, building the pleasure gradually until it feels like I'm going to burst if I don't come.

With one fist in the back of Maeve's hair and the other squeezing her ass, I press her down on me hard, hoping she's close.

Finally, when I think I won't last a second longer, Maeve throws her head back. Digging her fingernails into my shoulders, her lips part and she gasps what sounds like my name. She bounces a little faster, those beautiful tits jiggling in my face, right before her pussy starts clenching, pulsing around my shaft. She's so fucking sexy and having her orgasm on me feels like heaven. Finally, I let go of the tightly wound tension in my body, giving myself over to the ecstasy.

We're both still lost to the shuddering waves of pleasure when I hear a phone chiming off in the distance.

As our bodies begin to relax, Maeve collapses against me, and the noise gradually becomes louder and more frequent, ruining the most incredible sex of my life.

Maeve presses a kiss to my cheek and says, "You should probably answer that."

"That's me?" I ask since it hadn't even registered as my ringtone yet. And I can't say I even care who is calling when my deflating cock is still buried inside of its new favorite place in the world. I'm so big that I won't ever slip out. No, I'll stay right here until Maeve dismounts from me.

She doesn't yet, not even when she reaches down to dig into my jean pocket to pull the device free. Offering it to me, she finally, sadly, pulls my cock free so she can stand up.

I start to beg her to come back when I see the lit-up screen of my phone. "Huh," I mutter, finding I missed five calls from Nash. The only time Nash ever reaches out to me is if Malcolm's called a meeting. Since I just saw Malcolm banging his woman, I'm thinking a meeting is the last thing on his mind right now.

Nash calls again before I can listen to the multiple voicemails he also left.

"Yeah?" I answer, my voice still sounding lazy and sex drunk.

"Oh, thank fuck!" Nash exclaims in my ear. "Where have you been? I thought you were dead!"

"Dead?" I repeat in confusion.

"Some assholes just shot up the goddamn bar! Fiasco and Malcolm were hit, along with Hunt."

"What the fuck?" I shout in disbelief. "Someone shot up the bar!" I tell Maeve, who has her back to me as she slips her dress back on. Her shoulders stiffen before she looks over one and asks, "How bad is it?" which is my very next question for Nash.

"How bad is it?"

"Bad, worse for Fiasco, who took two bullets. But if we can find someone who knows how to remove the lead and sew them up, hopefully they'll live."

Hopefully? Did he just say, 'hopefully they'll live?'

"I'm on my way," I tell him in a rush.

"Wait! We need a vehicle, something to haul all three in, and fast before the cops show up!" he says. "Neighbors had to have heard the gunfire and called the police by now."

Why the fuck didn't I hear it? Oh, right, the sounds Maeve and I made were so loud and all-consuming that I doubt I would've heard an atomic bomb go off next door.

"On it," I promise him before ending the call. I learned how to hotwire a car before I could legally drive one. "We need a truck, big SUV, or a van," I tell Maeve as I put my pants on in record time. "Know of any in the area?"

"Ah, yeah," Maeve says. "There are usually a few of those in the apartment complex across the street."

"Good. Let's go."

She nods but doesn't say anything as I rush out the door and immediately start searching for a big vehicle. We're definitely in luck when I spot a big, red suburban across the street, exactly where Maeve mentioned one may be.

I jog over with her following behind me. And of course, the doors are locked.

"Shit!" I whisper. "I've got some electronics at the shop that could have this beast opened in no time. Unfortunately, we're going to have to do this the old-fashioned way. Maeve, stand by the back doors and keep watch while I work."

"What do you have to do exactly?" Maeve whispers, looking around nervously.

"I'm going to have to break the window, pop the hood, rip out the wiring to the horn to silence the alarm, then smash open the steering column and hotwire this thing."

"How long will that take?" Maeve asks.

I reply by drawing the long knife at my hip, then using it to shatter the driver's side window. The tinkling of glass as I clear the frame of the remnants of the window is drowned out by the honking of the horn as the alarm blares to life. I quickly reach in to unlock the door, pop the hood open, and then use my knife to sever the wiring to the horn.

"Anybody looking our way?" I ask as I slam the hood, then climb into the driver seat and begin working on the steering column.

"I don't see anybody..." Maeve begins, her face illuminated by the lights which are still flashing on the Suburban. "Shit!" she suddenly interjects as she runs around the truck, jumping into the passenger side. "There's an old guy with a key fob up on the top floor looking down here!" she says as she ducks down in the seat. She peeks out of the back window as I work on the wiring in the steering column, then lets out a long sigh. "He went back in, and I saw the lights flash on a car over there," she tells me. "He must have heard the racket and just been checking on his own car."

"Let's hope so," I grit out as I steel myself for the shock I know is incoming. I always give myself a jolt when doing this, and tonight is no different. I spark the starter module, and the engine roars to life. "Let's get the hell out of here!"

It takes less than a minute to get back to the bar. I pull up to the curb, and Maeve and I both jump out, leaving it running but in park. Several people are gathered together at the entrance of the alley between the bar and some sort of restaurant that's closed for the night. When I push my way through the bodies, I find Fiasco laid out on the pavement, several women holding shirts or dresses to his side and leg.

"Wirth!" he says when he looks up with heavy eyes and sees me. "I'm dying, man!"

Fuck!

"You're not dying. Load him up in the SUV while I find the others," I shout to the group who all look shell-shocked. "Move! Now!" I yell at them since I can already hear some sirens in the distance.

Rushing around to the door of the bar, I hurry inside, searching for Malcolm. The door is hanging open, littered with bullet holes.

There's shattered glass all around the bar, chairs are knocked over, and most of the tables have been overturned, probably because they tried to use the wooden furniture as shields.

I should've fucking been here!

"Wirth!" Nash calls me over to the area where I sat with Malcolm and Naomi just a few minutes before. He's standing with Devlin and Silas, all three of which have their guns drawn and ready.

"You find a car?" Nash asks me.

"Yeah," I say when I jog over and find a shirtless Malcolm. Naomi is standing beside him, tears streaming down her face while she holds his shirt to the wound on his shoulder.

"I can't believe this happened!" she sobs.

"I'm fine, honey," Malcolm grumbles. To me, he looks up and says, "It's just a scratch. Bullet went right through clean."

"A bullet! You took a bullet to the shoulder!" Naomi exclaims.

"He's going to be fine," Jetta assures her, taking over pressing down on the wound when Naomi breaks down, burying her face in her hands.

"We need to move," Nash says. "Can you walk?" he asks Malcolm.

"If you all would get the hell out the way, I would've been gone by now," our president says when he takes over holding the shirt to his shoulder. He gets to his feet and tries to push past Silas and Devlin.

"Go easy there, prez," Dev warns him before he and Silas take the lead to the door, guns still out and at the ready.

"Cops are on their way," I point out. "We need to get out of here, and fast."

Malcolm does seem fine, but there's a lot of blood soaking the shirt pressed to his bullet wound.

"We're coming too!" one of the former Knights — Preston I think is his name — calls out as he and the big boy, Titus, carry a limp Hunt to the door as he tries and fails to keep a towel up to his head. It slips down and reveals a bloody, gushing ear. Or what used to be an ear, I suppose.

"Damn," I mutter under my breath at the grizzly sight.

"Would've been fine...if someone...hadn't slammed my head...into the ground," Hunt murmurs.

"You didn't get shot again, did you?" Titus remarks.

"I want to come with him," Naomi says, but Malcolm shoots her down.

"You all need to get out of here and go home, check on the baby."

"I'll call them an Uber," Maeve says when she reappears, already on her phone.

"Thanks," I tell her, meaning for everything tonight.

We get all three of the men loaded up, Malcolm and Hunt in the back with Hunt's guy, Preston, next to him to help keep him upright. Fiasco went into the cargo hold so he could have more room to stretch out. The fact that we needed Devlin and Silas to squeeze in there with him to apply pressure is concerning as I hop in the driver seat and Nash climbs into the passenger seat after saying a quick goodbye to the women, despite Naomi's continued protest. At least she has the other women to stay with her.

"Where to?" I ask Nash. "We can't go to a hospital. Bullet wounds are reported to the police."

"Fuck. I don't know," Nash says. "Except, well, there is one possibility..."

"What is it?" I ask as I pull off down the road. "Which direction?"

"Back toward Carolina Beach," Nash replies. "Lucy found my sister."

"Okay. That's fucking great," I tell him as I take the exit ramp on the right so fast the SUV's left tires come off the ground. "But what the hell does your sister have to do with anything right now, man?"

"She's a nurse."

"Oh. And you think she'll help these guys?"

"I don't know," he says softly. "Haven't met her yet."

"Jesus Christ," I grumble.

"Now is as good a time as any, I guess. Let me see if Lucy has her number and can at least warn her that we're coming," Nash says as he fumbles for his phone and finally gets it up to his ear. He relays the message to his girl of what we need and then ends the call a second later.

"Well?" I ask.

"Lucy's texting me her address and will call her up to let her know we're coming," he responds.

Glancing over at him now that I'm on the straight shot highway going a hundred miles an hour, I whisper, "And what if she turns us away?"

"Fuck! I don't know," he exclaims, stabbing his fingers through his brown hair and giving it a tug before my eyes go back to the dark, empty road in front of me. "She'll just have to help us!"

"Right," I huff. "Because that's how you get the best medical care – hold someone at gunpoint and demand it."

"We're not going to hold her at gunpoint," Nash snaps.

"We're not? Even if she's our only option for saving Fiasco?"

"Dammit. I don't know, okay? Let's just pray she'll do it without it coming to that."

"Yeah, let's hope."

"Ah, guys," Malcolm says from behind Nash's seat, so I quickly glance over my shoulder and find Hunt slumped against his side. "I don't know where we're going but make it fast. Hunt's out cold."

"Shit, I'm going as fast as this big tank will go, prez," I say when I press the pedal down to the floorboard. "We needed a car to haul people; and unfortunately, big ones can't go zero to sixty in three seconds."

"Take the next exit," Nash tells me as he stares down at his phone. "We're only about five minutes away."

"Where is five minutes away?" Malcolm grumbles, which tells me all I need to know about his health. If he is his normal grouchy self, barking orders, then he is going to be fine.

"My sister's place," Nash swivels around in his seat to inform him.

"I didn't know you had a sister," Malcolm replies.

"I, ah, haven't actually met her yet."

"Well, fuck," Malcolm huffs, echoing my sentiments.

If we're wrong about Nash's long-lost sister, then we could be signing Fiasco's death warrant and possibly Hunt's.

"How's he doing back there, guys?" I call out to Silas and Devlin who have been quiet.

"Fiasco's taking a little nap," Silas says. "Sure, he'll be just fine."

"His pulse is weak," Devlin admits. "He's losing a shit ton of blood."

"Hold pressure," Malcolm tells them. "Tighter!"

"We're almost there. Hopefully," I call back to them.

"Who the fuck did this?" Malcolm asks Hunt's guy, Preston.

"They had on masks, so I can't be certain," he starts. "But we have heard that the Irish aren't happy about us coming to town."

"The Irish?" Nash repeats. "Bikers, gang, or mafia?"

"Mafia."

"Why the fuck didn't you tell us that before tonight?" Malcolm yells at him.

"We just heard some gossip around town, nothing concrete! It's not like they sent us a note telling us they were going to shoot up the place!"

"From now on, I need to know everything, even whispers. You hear me?" Malcolm growls.

"Yes, sir." After several quiet moments as I take more directions from Nash, putting the SUV on two wheels a few more times, Preston goes on to say, "If we lose Hunt, we won't have enough for a fucking chapter."

"You're not going to lose Hunt," Malcolm grunts.

"You've got a prospect, don't you?" I ask him.

"How the fuck did you know that?" Preston mutters.

"Why the fuck didn't I?" Malcolm shouts at him.

"Yeah, we've got a prospect, but he's too green. It hasn't even been three months yet!"

The rest of the way the SUV is quiet following that comment – too quiet as we all retreat into our own heads.

Finally, after what feels like a lifetime, we pull up outside of a small white, one-story cottage. It's in the cul-de-sac of a regular, lower-middle class neighborhood in a good part of town.

"We're here," I announce to the other guys as if it wasn't obvious. "How we gonna do this?"

"You and I will go to the door with Malcolm if he thinks he can walk," Nash says.

"I can fucking walk!" our president declares before he's pushing open his door and jumping out with Nash and I right behind him. The two of them are halfway up the paved sidewalk by the time I walk around the front hood of the SUV, so I have to jog to catch up to them when they're already ringing the doorbell.

A few long seconds later, the main door opens and a woman in a blue robe stands on the other side of a glass storm door, the entry way behind her lit up. Just a glimpse, and it's easy to see the resemblance to Nash in her lean face, her long, chocolate brown hair frizzy from the pillow and her golden eyes confused and…scared.

"Ah, hi," Nash says to her calmly through the glass, realizing the same thing I have. "Sorry to bother you so late, but we're desperate here. I think my girlfriend Lucy called you…"

"How did you find me? H-how did you know I'm a nurse and where I live?" she asks, her voice shaky and words muffled by the glass.

"That's a long story for another time. Can you please help my friends? All he needs is a few stiches," he tells her, pointing to Malcolm. "But um, two of our other friends are in bad shape in the SUV."

Her gaze goes around us to the vehicle sitting at the curb.

"Your girlfriend warned me there were three patients," she says as she thankfully unlocks the glass door to open it for us. "That's more than I can handle on my own, so I called a friend. She's on the way. Until then, I'm going to need your help."

"Okay, I'll do whatever you need. Thank you, Joanna," Nash says with an exhale of relief.

# CHAPTER SEVEN

*Maeve*

The bar is a mess.

Several of the Knights are arguing with the officers out front like they're trying to keep them out of the building, so I sneak into the back. Inside, several other girls are sweeping up and wiping up blood stains while crying. I get to work helping them, feeling awful and worried about the three injured men. While I'm praying for them, especially Hunt and what his loss would mean to the club, all I can think about is murder.

I'm going to fucking kill Cormac.

That asshole and my brother told me that it was just going to be a quick drive-by to try and scare the MC out of town.

Instead of just messing up the building or the bikes, they nearly killed three men and could've easily hurt one of the innocent women during their stupid ass shootout.

But then later on in the night, when the police finally force their way inside to inventory evidence and make everyone sit down until they have a chance to interview us, I overhear two of the former Knights talking about the shooting and how they hoped they hit one of the masked bastards that came into the bar.

I jump up out of my chair so fast it falls over backward, hitting the floor and setting off a loud *BOOM* that startles everyone, especially the cops.

"Sorry," I say as I pick the chair back up again while everyone is staring at me. "It's been an awful night. Can I please leave? I told you I wasn't even here when the shooting happened."

The nearest cop gives a nod of approval.

"You need someone to walk you back to your apartment?" Bernard, the bartender, asks.

I inwardly cringe at his consideration since he has no idea I'm to blame for the club's president getting shot and nearly killed. Hopefully Hunt makes it. He's wild and a little unhinged when it comes to fucking, but he's a good man deep down. "Thank you for the sweet offer, but I'm sure I'll be fine," I tell him.

As soon as I step out of the bar, I spot a police cruiser riding slowly down the street, keeping an eye out on the area to make sure no other violence goes down.

I let myself into my apartment and hear the television, telling me I'm not alone. It's a huge relief to know he's okay since he was going to be the first person I called when I got home, but that doesn't mean I'm not angry at him.

"How could you?" I yell at my brother with tears filling my eyes before I even find him lounging on my sofa like he lives here and wasn't just involved in a horrifying shooting.

"Your intel was spot on, sis," Rian says with a grin when he turns his attention from the television to me fuming with my arms crossed over my chest. "We had no idea that the Dirty Aces were coming to town to patch the Knights over before your tip. Hopefully we got to them before that went down. The last thing we need are the Knights growing bigger, having more protection."

"You almost killed three people! There were innocent women in there!" I say as I stomp over and slap the shit out of his face, leaving my palm stinging. What I really want to do is punch him hard enough to knock the smugness out of his body, but I know from experience that my brother throws the "no hitting a girl" rule out the window if I attack first.

I hate to see him like this, turning into our father a little more each day.

Instead of getting up to hit me back, Rian simply rubs at his cheek and says, "Almost killed them? Shit, the leaders aren't dead?"

"I-I don't know," I admit as I drop onto the opposite side of the sofa, as far away from him as I can get and bury my face in my hands. "No one at the bar has heard from them yet…" I murmur into my palms.

"So, there's still hope," Rian cheerfully responds. "Cormac said that if we take out the leaders, the leftover members may try to plan some sort of retaliation. We'll be ready for them if they do. All they'll accomplish is killing enough of their own guys that they'll be forced to fold up the Wilmington chapter and go back to where they came from."

Lifting my face from my hands, I yell, "Cormac is a fucking fool! He's going to get you killed!"

"No, he's not. I can take care of myself."

"That's what you think," I mutter. "Were you there tonight? Were you one of the shooters?"

"Fuck yeah, I was. I hit the long-haired bastard, the president of the Dirty Aces."

"You better hope they all live; because if any of them die, they will come after you hard."

He casually stretches both of his arms across the top of the sofa. "And, like I just said, we'll be ready."

"This isn't you, Rian! You're better than this – acting like some maniac with a gun attacking people. What will it take for you to finally realize that Cormac is just trying to get you killed? He's never going to give up power to you!"

"Yes, he will," Rian responds through gritted teeth. "When I'm twenty-one, I'll take over and he'll be my second."

"Oh my god. You are so delusional," I say with a shake of my head. "He'll kill you himself before you ever reach twenty-one!"

"I trust Cormac with my life. Dad trusted him too. He would never betray me."

"Whatever you say, baby brother," I sigh as I lean my head back. "Just promise me that if you get even an inkling that he's coming after you, that you'll tell me, and we'll leave. Please? Don't try and fight him on your own."

"It'll never come to that," he says.

But what he doesn't know is that Cormac and I have our own deal. He made me a promise, and he can't back out. I refuse to let him. Once the Knights are out of town, he'll find a way to run Rian out of the Irish chaos once and for all.

If he doesn't live up to his promise, then I'll kill him myself if that's what it takes to save Rian from certain death.

*Wirth*

IT TAKES a few minutes to get everyone inside and situated in the small house. Most of us are hanging around in the kitchen out of the way. Fiasco is laid out in Joanna's bedroom and Hunt is stretched out on her sofa. Nash and Preston assist Joanna as she runs back and forth from one room to the other until another woman about the same age comes busting through the door without knocking, nearly giving us all a heart attack before she takes over the duties on Hunt.

Malcolm's sitting at the small, four-person dining table in the corner of the kitchen with a bandage on his shoulder. Joanna gave me the gauze, tape, and some antiseptic after checking the wound, and let me slap the prez back together.

Hunt's guy, Preston, comes over, wiping the sweat from his brow a little while later. "She thinks Hunt has a concussion and that the throbbing of his headache made the side of his head bleed more. He's going to be fine, she said, but he lost the top half of his ear."

"Jesus," I mutter.

"Casey!" Joanna yells from the bedroom. "I need you in here if you can leave him!"

"On my way," the other woman calls back before she disappears.

"That's not good," Silas says when he takes a seat in one of the three empty chairs at the table with Malcolm. "Nash is still in there too."

"I'll go check on things," I say since I can't sit still, and pacing isn't doing any good.

I head around the corner and down the short hall to the bedroom. Inside, Nash's sister is sitting on the bed next to Fiasco with a tube going from her arm to his as he sleeps. Her friend Casey slowly and methodically pulls a needle and thread through the skin of his leg. Nash is just standing and watching.

"He needed blood," Joanna looks up and says when she sees me. "I'm O positive, so I hope he's positive and not negative. Either way he was screwed."

"Yeah, let's hope he's positive," I reply.

"Joanna didn't see any internal damage on his side and got him stitched up there," Nash explains. "She pulled the bullet from his leg, and Casey is closing him up."

"Now we just have to find some antibiotics to give him to make sure he doesn't get an infection." Joanna places her hand on Fiasco's forehead. "He already feels warm. Can infection start this soon?"

"Anything is possible," Casey replies without looking up from her sewing.

With each of her new stabs, Fiasco's face winces.

Noticing, Joanna says, "We need better pain meds too."

Casey pauses and looks at the other woman in concern.

"He's tough. He can take it," Nash says. "Better to have the pain than bleed to death, right?"

"Right," Casey agrees before she goes back to work.

"So, um, now that things have calmed down, I think it's a good time for that long story of yours," Joanna says to Nash.

"Oh, well, ah, where to start?" he looks to me, eyes wide in question like he expects me to know what to say here.

"Go on," Joanna encourages him. Nash opens his mouth to say something and then shuts it again, shoulders slumping. He's obviously not ready to tell her she's his sister yet. So, I try to jump in and help him out.

"Nash's girlfriend is a computer genius. We were in the area and needed medical attention for the guys but couldn't take them to the hospital," I explain.

Nash nods at me and then picks up the story. "So, Lucy, that's my girlfriend, she pulled up the state's nursing board or whatever to find someone close and there you were."

"Huh," Joanna mutters. "And why couldn't you take them to the hospital exactly?"

"There was a shooting," Nash tells her. "We were attacked at a bar and have no idea who it was yet, but we like to handle that type of thing ourselves, without getting law enforcement involved."

"Right," she drawls. "And bullet wounds are reported to law enforcement when they show up in the ER."

"Yes, exactly!" Nash replies. "But we didn't hurt anyone. Or at least, I don't think we did. When the men barged in with masks on, some people fired back to make them retreat. We're innocent, though."

"Uh-huh," Casey mutters as she clips the thread. "You all look… innocent in your little motorcycle vests."

"Cuts," I correct her. "They're cuts. And we're in a motorcycle club. That's all they are."

"Sure. Whatever you say," Joanna replies as her and her friend exchange a look.

"We owe you both for helping," Nash tells them. "Name your price and we'll pay it; just please don't tell anyone we were here."

"I don't know about Casey, but I don't want to lose my nursing license. My mouth will remain shut."

"Mine too," Casey responds. "And I think…a thousand for each of us would be sufficient."

"A thousand? That would work for me," Joanna agrees.

"No," Nash tells them, and I'm about to smack him for refusing their offer when he goes on to add, "Five thousand at least. For each of you. It's the least we can do."

"That's very generous of you," Joanna says when she smiles at him. It's a flirty smile. Jesus. She has no fucking idea. Nash really should tell her that they're biologically related.

"No, ah, what you're doing is generous," Nash stammers, rubbing at the back of his neck after he picks up on the same vibe. "I should go check on Malcolm and Hunt," he tells them before escaping the room. Joanna's eyes follow him.

Since he doesn't want to spill the beans yet about their connection, I decide to remind her, "He has a girlfriend he's crazy about. She's a tiny little thing that's vicious when she needs to be."

"And?" Joanna says as she narrows her eyes at me in question.

"And I'm just putting that out there."

"Like I would ever be interested in some criminal outlaw biker dude," Joanna responds. She tries to point her finger to her chest which tugs on the tube connecting her to Fiasco, making her wince when she has to readjust the entry point in her skin. "No, thank you. I have enough problems on my own."

"Good," I reply. "Not that I'm glad you have problems but that you wouldn't waste your time…Whatever. I'm going to check on the other guys," I say so I can get the hell out of there before I blurt out Nash's secret. "Just take care of him, okay?" I tell her with a nod of my chin at Fiasco's prone form on the bed.

"I'll do my best," Joanna says before I walk back into the living room.

## CHAPTER EIGHT

*Maeve*

I don't sleep at all after my brother finally leaves. I just lie in bed angry at myself for being a part of Cormac's ploy that hurt three men.

It's been years since I've been to church. I haven't been since my father used to make me attend Mass like a good, little, Catholic girl. Eventually, when I was old enough to call him out on his hypocrisy of being a church-going mob boss, he stopped making me go.

But this morning, when I give up on sleep, I get up, take a quick shower, and then go to the chapel to get on my knees and pray to God that those men live.

I may have only known Hunt for a few weeks, but we've been as close as two humans can get many times. At first, I was just playing the part, trying to get on the inside to give Cormac information. But Hunt and some of the other men grew on me. I would consider Hunt a friend, and I know he would protect me and the other club girls from anything.

Then there's Wirth's two friends. I can't imagine what he's going through, seeing them both injured. The one outside took two bullets and left puddles of blood behind on the concrete in the alley. He's probably the one who will struggle the most to overcome his injuries.

Once I finish my prayer, I go over to the votive stand and light four candles – three for the injured men and one for my brother's soul. Rian is so hard-headed and cocky, like my father. He thinks he was born to lead. That path will only end with him in the ground, losing his life before he ever gets to have one.

If my brother can't be reasoned with, that means I have to go to someone who will.

Cormac.

Since my car is still busted up on the side of the highway, I have to take the bus to get to the Irish pub on the other side of town.

I bust through the front door and start down the hall toward Cormac's office where a gigantic man with a shaved head that I've never seen before is standing guard.

"I need to see Cormac."

"He's not to be disturbed," the man replies with a voice so deep I can barely make out the words.

"Too bad," I tell him when I slip around him and try the doorknob. Since it's locked, I bang my fist on the door while yelling, "Cormac! Let me in! We need to talk!"

"He's not in his office," the giant informs me. "He's still asleep."

"How can he be asleep after what he did last night?" I demand, going down the hallway and banging on each and every door until one finally opens and the asshole steps out...tying the belt on his maroon silk robe that I'm guessing has nothing under it.

"Feeling fancy this morning after a night of attempted murder?" I snap at him.

"Maeve, it's too fucking early for your dramatics. Come back later," Cormac says as he rubs his hand over his bearded jaw and then his temple like I'm giving him a headache.

"How could you let my brother do your dirty work last night? He could've been killed!"

"He was wearing a bullet-proof vest," he replies.

"Was there one on his head too? Because if there wasn't, all it would take is one shot to kill him!"

Groaning and refusing to even look at me, Cormac says, "Jesus. Do you think I'm that reckless with my men? He was also wearing a helmet."

"Oh. Well, that's still not good enough," I tell him. "Are you trying to get him killed? Have you decided that would be the easiest way to get rid of him?"

"I'm not going to get your brother killed," he says simply. "But he's not a child anymore. He wants to be a part of this, and you have no right to try and stop him."

I gasp indignantly. Lowering my voice, I remind him, "Oh no. No, Cormac! We have a deal, remember? You promised me that once the Knights were gone, he was gone!"

"That was before I knew the Knights were getting protection from a bigger MC! Getting rid of the Knights now is going to require more bloodshed."

"I hate you," I tell him through my gritted teeth. "You're going to end up getting Rian killed; and when you do, I'm going to come after you!"

Suddenly, I'm hefted off of my feet and am dangling from the air thanks to an arm banded around my waist.

"Show her out, Cletus," Cormac says to the giant.

"We weren't done talking!" I exclaim when I am turned around against my will, and then we're headed to the door.

"Yes, we were," Cormac says while I'm carried outside and dropped.

"Don't come back, Miss Maeve. I don't want to have to hurt you," the giant says before he slams the door in my face.

"Assholes!" I shout.

∼

*Wirth*

"I NOW CALL this joint meeting of the original Dirty Aces and the new Wilmington Dirty Aces to order," Malcolm says without the least bit of enthusiasm. We're all tired after a long-ass, bloody night. Fiasco and Hunt are still at Joanna's house, in too much pain to make it to our pool hall. I think Hunt's issue is more vanity than anything now that he's missing a huge chunk of his ear. He doesn't have to say it for us all to know he feels guilty, like he should've done more to protect his people and ours.

"Let me go ahead and say what everyone else is thinking," Nash starts. Looking to the four new Wilmington members at the other end of the table, he says, "You guys may have a rat problem."

"Are you fucking kidding?" Preston yells. "How do we know you all don't have a rat?"

Malcolm slams down his gavel so loudly on the wooden table that I feel it echo in my skull. "Shut your fucking mouth now or take off those cuts," he tells the new guys. "We're trying to help. One of your men was shot, yeah, but two of us were fucking hit."

"So, you're saying we have a rat because we had less injured?" Titus grunts. "Maybe our men are just faster at ducking."

"Watch it!" Malcolm warns him, narrowing his eyes and pointing the gavel in his direction like he's considering slamming it against his big head. "I got winged when I was protecting my woman. Fiasco was outside in the open, unprotected. He couldn't have just *ducked* to avoid getting shot twice!"

"Sorry," Titus mutters, his enormous shoulders slumping inward after being chastised.

"Tell us more about these Irish fuckers that you failed to mention before patching over. Preston said you've heard rumors the Irish weren't happy with you taking up residence in Wilmington," Malcolm explains.

"You know how people talk shit," Troy says. "That's all we thought it was – talk. If we had any idea they would come at us like that, we would've told you."

"Even if it is the Irish, how would they have known that we were there too? Doesn't seem like the attack was a coincidence, does it?" Silas asks.

"You think someone tipped them off," I say in understanding.

"It wasn't our guys!" Preston exclaims.

"Yeah, we would know if we had a traitor," Titus adds. "What about him?" He points his sausage finger in my direction so suddenly that I feel like I've got whiplash.

"What about me, motherfucker?" I hit back.

"You weren't there when the shooting started," Titus explains. "That doesn't seem like a coincidence."

"I will ram this gavel up your ass if you ever insinuate that it was one of my men again," Malcolm warns him, but I can take up for myself.

"You and Hunt know goddamn well where I was," I tell Titus. "You're just pissed because Maeve left with me and didn't go upstairs with you. Get the hell over it. Just because I was getting fucked and you weren't doesn't make me a traitor."

"Why didn't she take you upstairs like usual? Picked the perfect time to vanish. Did you ask her to leave?" he remarks.

"No. Maeve wanted to go back to her place. It was right down the street. Not my fault if she's never invited you to her bed. Then again, I wasn't the one trying to drag her upstairs regardless of what she wanted."

Titus growls but doesn't get to say whatever he wanted to say when Nash holds up his hand and then chimes in.

"Hold on. Start from the beginning." Then to me he says, "You left the bar with one of their girls?"

"Yes. Maeve. I actually gave her a ride to the bar after finding her trying to change her tire on the exit ramp."

Shit, that reminds me that I need to get a tow truck out to get her car before the Highway Patrol moves it. With everything going on, I had forgotten all about that.

"Is she trustworthy?" Nash asks. It's the first time I've ever wanted to pound in his pretty face.

"She's fucked all of them, so they know her better than I do," I grit out.

"Maeve's a sweetheart," Preston says, speaking of her fondly. "She's loyal to the core."

I can feel Malcolm, Nash, Silas, and Devlin watching me, waiting for my take. They're all thinking the same thing, can we really trust the woman just because she's a club slut?

"She showed me a hell of a good time and didn't seem the least bit nervous or on edge," I assure them.

"Good. Then we'll forget about her," Malcolm says, which is a relief. "Who else is a club girl or hang around?" he asks the guys while in my gut, something unsettling is trying to twist up my insides.

Everything happened so fast last night, especially once we got back to Maeve's place. But I can't forget how adamant she was about leaving the bar – first to go to the store and then to take me to her place. Was she trying to leave because she knew shit was going to go down?

I don't hear the rest of the guys talking during the meeting as I replay every second of the night from the very beginning.

What if there was more to Maeve seducing me, insisting we leave, than I want to believe?

It's not like I'm going to voice that shit aloud to Malcolm and the others, because there's no telling what they would do to try and make her talk.

No, I need to have proof first before I go and point a finger at anyone, especially a woman who could be completely innocent.

I'll just have to keep an eye on Maeve myself, get closer to her, and see what happens while I work on her car as promised.

But if she is the one responsible for telling the Irish about the Dirty Aces partying with the Knights, then I'll have no choice but to turn her over to the club.

Fuck, I hope I'm right about her.

"Now," Malcolm says with a slap of his palm on the table, bringing my attention back to the meeting. "Let's talk about how the fuck we're going to retaliate."

The men at the table cheer while all I can think about is Maeve.

# CHAPTER NINE

*Maeve*

Being alone in my apartment, isolated from the rest of the MC as the sun sets on one of the shittiest days ever really sucks. The bar is closed until further notice, and the men are all MIA. All I got was a short text from one of the other club girls telling me to avoid the bar until I'm specifically told otherwise, in case it gets hit again while the men are out of town.

When I asked about how everyone is doing, she said she didn't know. No one knows. The Knights have cut off communication with everyone, probably because they're worried about someone inside being a rat.

And they would be right.

But the reason I want to know how the men are doing is not to go and report back to Cormac. I'm genuinely worried about them. I never meant for this to happen, for anyone to get hurt. Cormac said they were just going to try and scare the Knights out of town, not attempt to murder them all.

Too nervous to sit still and with no car to ride around in, I'm stuck pacing near the front door, trying to decide if I try and catch a bus to…anywhere. Staying here alone is driving me crazy. That's when my phone suddenly begins to ring for the first time all day. I scramble to pull it out of my back jean pocket.

It's a number I don't recognize from Carolina Beach.

"Hello?" I answer quickly.

"Maeve?" a man's deep, rumbly voice asks.

"Yes? Wirth?" I take a guess, remembering I gave him my number last night when we were on the side of the road. If I had his, I would've already called him.

"Yeah," he says, sounding slightly annoyed for some unknown reason. "I just wanted to let you know that I had your car towed to my shop. I'll start working on it tonight."

"Thank you," I say in relief, glad to hear another human being's voice, one so kind and considerate. "But you don't have to work on it tonight," I tell him. "I'm guessing you've had a pretty stressful day. How is everyone?"

I hold my breath while I wait for him to respond. He's silent for an incredibly long time before he finally says, "Recovering."

"Good," I exhale in relief. "That's good. I'm so glad."

"Well, I just wanted to tell you I hadn't forgotten about your car," he says.

"I'm sorry about last night," I blurt out before pursing my lips to slow down before I say too much and end up getting myself killed along with my brother. "What I mean is, I'm sorry I was so rude to you when you were just trying to help me with my flat tire. There's no excuse for it. All I can say is that I've had some bad experiences with men over the years."

"Yeah, I don't doubt that," Wirth responds, sounding slightly less agitated. "Do you need a ride anywhere tomorrow?"

"No, I don't think so. Nowhere I have to be. I just, I hate being alone."

"You missing your guys? They won't be home for a while."

"Where are they? Is Hunt with you?" I ask.

"Can't tell you that," he says quickly, and I get the feeling that he doesn't trust me. He's a smart man as well as kind and hot as hell.

"Well, if you talk to them, tell them I've been praying for them."

"Really, you've been *praying* for them?" he scoffs like he thinks I'm lying or just giving him lip service.

"I have. I went to church today and also lit a candle for the three men that were injured."

"That's, ah, that's nice of you, I guess," Wirth stammers. Then, he goes on to ask, "Are you the only girl Hunt fucks?"

"What?" I ask since the question is so off topic and out of nowhere.

"Were you trying to be his old lady?" he rephrases.

"No. Of course not. Hunt isn't going to settle down with anyone ever. I may not have known him long, but I'm certain of that."

"What about the other men?"

"Just spending time with them. Having fun," I respond before I finally go and sit down on my sofa, giving my feet a break. "I'm sure you've had plenty of your own fun as a hot biker in the original Dirty Aces."

"Not as much as you think," he says, which I find incredibly hard to believe.

∼

Wirth

I'M STARTING to feel like an enormous dick for thinking badly of Maeve.

She sounds honestly concerned about how the guys are doing. The woman actually went to a church and prayed for them today.

Unless…what if she went to pray because she's feeling guilty? Isn't that what some church-goers do – go to church to ask God to forgive them for their sins?

"Well," Maeve says after declaring that she isn't serious about any of the Knights. "I think you had fun with me."

"I did," I agree. So much fun that I'm jealous of Hunt when all she did was mention his name. She's probably right that he doesn't want more with her. Hunt seemed happy enough to offer her up to me, even when his boy tried to take her upstairs last night.

"Do you maybe want to do it again sometime?" she asks.

My dick swells against the zipper of my jeans at just the thought, giving me his answer. The rest of me, especially my head, knows it's not a good idea after everything that went down, not until I know Maeve is trustworthy.

"Guess we'll see," I reply.

"Yeah, I guess we will," she agrees.

Fuck, this woman has had too much power over me since the second I saw her on her knees trying to change a tire on a goddamn hill. If I don't hang up with her soon, her sexy, raspy voice will have me getting on my bike and going to see her in the next five seconds.

"I need to go," I tell her. "I'll call you when I know more about your car."

"Oh. Okay," Maeve says, sounding surprised by my sudden attempt to end the call. "Thanks for everything, Wirth."

"Yeah, no problem," I respond. "Take care of yourself, Maeve."

"You too," she says softly before I end the call.

Staring at her banged up car under the bright lights of the empty, silent garage all afternoon makes it impossible for me to stop thinking about her.

I need to get out of here. Get some air.

Outside, I climb on my bike and race off toward Joanna's house to check on Fiasco and Hunt. I haven't heard from Malcolm or anyone in a few hours.

I'm not surprised when I pull up and see Nash's bike hiding parallel to a big, green bush next to the cement driveway. I push mine up next to his; because even though it's dark, there's no reason to leave my Yamaha out on the street for a nosy neighbor to get the license plate written down.

I send him a quick text before I go up to the door and scare the shit out of him or his sister. Nash comes to the door to open it rather than respond by return text.

"Hey, man. You coming to check on the guys?" he asks when he strolls out holding open the glass door, leaving the main door open for the light from inside to shine on the porch steps.

"Yeah. Haven't heard any updates in a while and was feeling antsy," I admit to him.

"Come on in. Fiasco's been in and out of sleep."

"Oh yeah? That's a good sign," I say when he turns to go back inside and I follow him, shutting and locking the deadbolt on the front door behind me.

"Hope Joanna doesn't mind another visitor tonight…" he trails off.

"How's that going?" I ask him quietly. "Have you, you know, told her yet?"

"Not yet," he whispers.

"What the hell are you waiting for, man?"

"I don't know," he says, turning around to face me. "I'm not sure how she'll react. Until Fiasco is out of here, I think it's best to not bring it up just yet."

"Yeah," I reply since I can't fault him for being worried about her kicking us all to the curb for keeping that secret.

"Joanna's in the bedroom with Fiasco if you want to go on in," he says.

I glance around the small house and ask, "Where's Hunt? He already left?"

"Ah, not exactly," Nash grumbles. "He's in the bathroom."

"He doing okay?"

"Oh yeah," he says with a grin. "If you listen closely, you can hear the sounds of just how much better he's feeling right now."

Once we stop talking, I can, in fact, hear a repetitive thumping sound and…soft moans from the hallway.

Nash clears his throat and says, "Joanna's friend, Casey, has been helping with Hunt's recovery in a multitude of ways."

"So, he is obviously feeling better. Good for him I guess." I'm also relieved because knowing Hunt's busy fucking another woman is even more proof that he doesn't have his heart set on Maeve. Or best of all, his dick.

"I'm going to see if Lucy can come give us a ride out of here once they're finished," Nash explains. "Unless Casey takes him home with her. Apparently, he was feeling self-conscious about the side of his head and ear being messed up. Joanna doesn't approve of her going this far to show him he's still, 'an attractive, virile man that women will want.'" Whispering, he adds, "I think my sister is a bit of a prude. Either that, or she thinks her and her friends are too good for bikers…"

"She's probably just being protective of her friend," I tell him.

"Yeah. Maybe," he agrees with a shrug. "Go on in and see Fiasco if you want. It's a little quieter in there with the door shut."

"Okay, thanks," I tell him when I start down the hall.

Turning the doorknob, I slip into the bedroom and apparently startle Joanna. The woman who was lying fully clothed on her side facing Fiasco suddenly sits up wide-eyed in surprise at seeing me.

"Jeez, you scared me," she says, clutching her chest.

"Sorry," I whisper. "Nash told me to come on in. How's he doing?" I nod my chin to the big, blond, shirtless man lying prone next to her, taking up more than half of her queen bed, sound asleep.

She lies back down with her head propped up on her arm facing him. "He's in and out. Mostly out. When he wakes up, he's in pain, so I give more morphine."

"Lucky you had that here."

"I had a friend steal it from the hospital pharmacy," she responds without looking at me.

"Oh."

"I took tomorrow off to keep an eye on him."

"Thank you," I tell her. "We really appreciate you helping him, even though you don't know us."

"You didn't really leave me much of a choice," she says with a smile when she turns to face me. "But the money was a nice and much needed surprise for me and Casey both."

"Yeah, and it looks like your friend is breaking her own rule," I remark, jutting my thumb over my shoulder in the direction of the bathroom.

"Sexual healing is a real thing. Or so Casey believes," she jokes.

"Oh yeah? Then maybe you should try that with Fiasco," I tease. "Nothing would get him up faster than a woman's touch."

"Not going to happen," she says with a shake of her head before she goes back to staring at him. "Well, not unless he gets worse. He is incredibly handsome."

"What God gave him in looks he took from his IQ," I say with a chuckle.

"That's just mean!" she whispers.

"It's the truth. Just wait until he wakes up," I tell her.

*Fuck, I really hope he wakes up.*

And until then, I'm going to do all I can to find out who is responsible for hurting him.

## CHAPTER TEN

*Maeve*

There's a loud knock on my door the next afternoon while I'm doing laundry to pass the time. I have no doubt it's my brother since I'm assuming the Knights are all still out of town.

I'm not really in the mood to deal with Rian, not after he and Cormac lied to me, but that's the thing about family – you have to love them even when you hate them.

Making sure it is, in fact, my brother, I put my eye up to the peephole; and all it takes is a flash of his auburn hair for me to start unlocking the door.

"You need to stop coming by here," I say when I jerk it open. "One of the Knights or girls could see you."

"Hello to you too, sis," he huffs before pushing right past me, inviting himself inside.

"Have you forgotten that I'm also still pissed at you," I say while shutting and locking the door. "No, not pissed, furious!" I then follow him into the kitchen where he starts going through the refrigerator like he lives here. "Since when did you become as bloodthirsty as dad?" I ask him.

Slamming the fridge door, he spins around to look at me. "Did one of them die?"

"I don't know! And how could you wish that on anyone?"

"They're trouble. Everyone knows it, especially you since you were up close and personal with them for weeks. But do you hear that sound?" he asks, putting his hand up to his ear.

"Hear what?" I ask, bracing my hands on my hips.

"Silence. No motorcycles revving. It's peaceful again in our neighborhood."

"They will be back, Rian. I bet they're plotting against you right now, you idiot! They won't go away that easily."

"So, where are they? Who are they plotting with?" he asks, grabbing an apple from my fruit bowl and taking a bite out of it.

"I-I don't know."

"Bullshit," he says between bites. "Are you seriously going to lie to your own brother to protect those dirty sons of bitches?"

"I'm not lying," I tell him through gritted teeth. "And you have no idea what I've done for you and Cormac!"

"Oh, please, Maeve," he says with a roll of his eyes. "Don't act like you were some kind of saint before the night you stepped into that bar."

"Yeah, you're right," I snap at him. "It's hard to be a saint when our father auctioned off my virginity to the highest bidder when I was sixteen!"

Rian freezes with his half-eaten apple halfway to his mouth. "No, he didn't."

"Really? You think I would lie about something like that?"

"He was a hardass, sure, but he wouldn't go that far…"

"He would and he did!" I shout at him. "There's a reason why he wouldn't let me date in high school. He made ten grand on my first time. Stood right outside the door of one of the hotel rooms down the street and listened, timing him! He gave him one hour to take my virginity."

Shaking his head, he says, "I don't believe that. You were daddy's little girl. If anything, he was overprotective of you to keep you safe."

I scoff because he's so fucking naïve. "Dad took the payment in cash and then listened, but did nothing when I was screaming for the man to stop. He had to have heard me sobbing when he didn't." Tears fill my eyes, and I try and hold them back. They didn't help me then, and they won't do anything to change what happened now. "The first man to undress me, to-to touch me, was some stranger! Our father took my innocence from me that night. So yeah, after that, sleeping around with whomever didn't really seem like a big deal."

Rian opens his mouth and then closes it before finally he says, "If that happened, I'm sorry."

"It did happen!" I scream at him. And the anger is what has the tears racing down both of my cheeks.

"Then I'm sorry, dammit! What else do you want me to say? Dad's dead, so I can't kick his ass for it. Why didn't you tell me when it happened?"

"Because you were only ten," I remind him. "You didn't even know what sex was yet."

"Oh," he mutters.

"And I don't want your pity. That's not why I told you now," I explain. "I just want you to be different from him. Don't become an evil asshole that finds joy in shooting people and hurting them, okay? That's why I've slept with all of the Knights, to help you!"

"I didn't ask you to do all that," is his response. "I would never ask you to whore yourself out."

"No, you didn't ask me to whore myself out," I agree with a sigh, ready to drop the entire conversation. He doesn't get it, and I can't tell him that Cormac is going to find a way to push him out because of our deal.

Swiping away the dampness from my cheeks with my fingers, I say, "Could you please leave now, or are you going to stay and eat the rest of my food?"

"Not like you don't have plenty of cash to buy more groceries," Rian responds, still pissed that I have access to my trust fund dad left but he won't until he's twenty-one and more responsible, if that day ever comes. If it's up to me, he'll at least live to see his twenty-first birthday, and many more after.

"Right, like a few hundred thousand can make up for the hell he put me through," I mutter before going over to my purse. I pull out all of the cash from my wallet and then take it to him. "Here."

"Thanks, sis," he says as he accepts and pockets the money. "Let me know if you hear any updates about the Knights."

"Yeah, sure," I say, even though I know I won't as I show him out the door.

It was one thing to try and help Cormac to save my brother, but I won't keep doing it if it means other people get hurt or killed.

There's enough guilt on my shoulders that three men were shot. And I'll have to live with that blame for the rest of my life. I don't think I could handle the burden of anyone's death on my conscience, not even to save Rian.

Maybe it was crazy for me to think I could save him at all.

∽

## Wirth

"Fuck," I mutter aloud when I see a man come strolling out of Maeve's apartment. Wouldn't you know it, the fellow looks like he has reddish-brown hair, although it's hard to tell from this far away.

I had been sitting on my bike on the other side of the complex watching through my binoculars for almost two hours when the fucker showed up.

It felt stupid when I first got here, spying on a woman who has been nothing but amazing to me and the other guys.

But now I'm glad I did it.

The potentially redhaired man could have some sort of connection to the Irish. That would just be too big of a coincidence if not, right?

He climbs into a black sedan, and I'm about to start my motorcycle to follow him when my phone buzzes in my pocket.

Pulling it out, I answer without looking at the screen with a curt, "What?"

"Wirth?" her sexy, raspy voice is so unique I know it's Maeve. Fuck, why the hell is she calling me?

"What's up?" I ask, wondering if she's somehow spotted me. "I'm kind of busy at the moment."

Then I hear her sniffle before she says, "I'm sorry to bother you, but I just, I wasn't sure who else to call and was wondering if you could come over."

*Goddammit.*

What if she's being manipulated by the ginger, forced to give the Irish intel?

"Did he hurt you?" I blurt out as I squeeze my eyes shut. "I mean, did someone hurt you?"

"No, nothing like that," she says before adding, "Well, not recently. I just don't want to be alone tonight."

"What does that mean?" I ask.

"Nothing. Forget it. I'm sorry I called. I'll let you go," she says in a rush.

"Wait!" I shout to stop her before she goes. "I'll come over," I agree. I do want to see her face, to figure out what's going on with her and the ginger and to make sure she's okay. "I'm, ah, actually in the area. The Knights needed someone at the bar for a, um, a delivery," I lie to explain why I'm already here in town.

"Oh. Okay. If you're sure?"

"I'll see you in a few," I tell her before ending the call. "Shit," I grumble to myself, wondering what the hell I'm doing.

I need to tell someone my suspicions about Maeve, but I could have it all wrong and then she would pay the price.

It's probably stupid, and could even be some sort of setup, but I can't stop myself from cranking up my bike and driving around the block a few times before finally pulling into a parking spot in her complex.

Climbing off my bike, I decide to send Malcolm a quick text.

*I'm at Maeve's in Wilmington if you need me.*

His response is nearly instantaneous, **The fuck you telling me for?**

*Just in case you need me*, I reply again with a grin before I slip my phone into my pocket and make my way to her door.

I've barely knocked when she yanks it open. She throws her arm around my neck so fast that I don't even have a chance to see her face. For all I know, some random woman could be hugging me. But then I inhale her strawberry and vanilla scent and know for certain it's her.

"Hey, are you okay?" I ask when she doesn't seem inclined to let go.

"Yeah, sorry." She gives a small laugh before finally letting go and taking a step backward to let me inside. In that second, I notice her eyes are red like she's been crying. "It's just nice to see you again."

Before I can ask any other questions, she's shut the door and then she's grabbing my face to pull my lips down to her sexy mouth.

"Slow down there, doll. What's the hurry?" I ask even as my hands move down her back to squeeze her amazing ass through her cotton shorts, ready to tear them and her t-shirt off to get to her curves.

"I just, I need you," she says with her palms sliding down my chest along the opening of my cut.

"Need me?" I repeat. Fuck, it's hard to keep my head on straight when she says shit like that, making my throat tighten and my dick throb and lengthen in my jeans so fast I get dizzy from the blood loss.

I try and tell myself that she's just like every other woman and that it's just sex – a much-needed release.

But fuck if it doesn't feel different when I'm near her – like there's a gravitational pull I can't fight no matter how hard I may try, just like the first night we were together. Not that I've tried to resist all that much.

Maeve knows how to push all of my buttons in the best fucking way. The woman is addictive. And if I'm not careful, I may lose myself in her and lose sight of the reason why I'm here in the first place – because I can't trust her. The Dirty Aces can't trust her.

I just saw with my own eyes a man leaving her place, a ginger who may prove that she's not loyal. That should be enough to make me push her away, but it's not.

Of course I still want to ask her who the fuck the man who left her apartment was, if he's hurting her, if she's fucking him.

I figure out a roundabout way of finding out the answer to the second question. Sliding my fingers down the back of her shorts and through her wet slit, I push two inside of her, making her gasp. "Are you sore?" I ask.

"Sore?" she repeats. "From last night?"

"Yeah," I reply as my lips and tongue feast on her neck while my fingers pump in and out of her pussy. "Or today? Earlier tonight?"

"What? I-I haven't been with…anyone…since you…" she trails off as her walls tighten around my fingers.

"Oh yeah?"

"Yeah," she answers in a sigh when I feel her getting closer and closer to coming; and for some stupid reason, I believe her. "W-what about you?"

"What about me?" I ask. My teeth nip at her sensitive flesh below her ear. The move makes her pussy clench in response.

"Have you…been with anyone?"

"No," I say, smiling against her skin because of her question and from being able to feel her reaction to my mouth on her, getting her worked up just as much as my fingers fucking her. She's gasping and moaning, her lower body squirming as she fists my cut, desperate for a release.

Wanting to get her there so I can finally get inside of her, I jerk her shorts and panties down her legs while pulling her shirt over her head, leaving her beautifully naked. As soon as Maeve steps out of her bottoms, I grab her by her thighs, lifting her up so that her legs wrap around my waist.

"Bed. Now," she urges before her mouth finds mine. I'm on board with that plan.

I shove three fingers into her pussy from behind as I kiss her, then stumble my way through the living room, searching for a bedroom while Maeve tries to get my cut off.

There's a light coming from a back room, so I head in that direction, thankful when I see the neatly made queen bed from the door.

I toss Maeve down on the mattress long enough to get my clothes off and put a condom on. She's too stunning to be real lying on her back waiting for me, her eyelids heavy with lust as she watches me.

"Damn. Why didn't I get you naked last night?" Maeve asks.

"I was too impatient to undress," I admit as I pounce on top of her, crawling up her body until our mouths meet. Our lips and tongues are just as frantic as our bucking lower bodies to join. My plan to get her off on my fingers goes out the window as soon as I feel the heat of her pussy through the latex.

It's not an easy fucking fit. Noticing my difficulty, Maeve reaches down to guide me inside while spreading her thighs as wide as she can to take me.

"God, yes," she moans as I sink in those first few amazing inches. Her eyes drift closed and her lips part in a silent scream as I fill her up.

Nothing else matters at that moment in time but the woman under me. Everything else is forgotten. I couldn't even spell my name because letters and language cease to exist.

It's just me and Maeve, nearly every inch of the front of our bodies touching and moving in sync. I try to go slow to savor the pleasure, make it last, and not hurt her. But then Maeve's fingernails dig into my ass cheeks before she says against my lips, "More. Faster. Please."

I push my upper body off of hers, bracing my palms on either side of her head to look down at her face. "You sure?"

Maeve nods and then gives a verbal answer. "Yes. Don't hold back," she says.

So, I don't.

I finally let go and let my body have whatever it needs, what it's been needing for years, maybe for my entire life. I've always been too careful with the few women I was with to take it from them. My hips pound into Maeve relentlessly while I stare down into her green eyes that are holding me captive.

*"Oh God, Wirth! Yes! YES!"*

Every word from her mouth is encouraging me to keep going, while her pussy does the same, her inner walls clenching and releasing around my cock faster and faster, pulling me impossibly deeper into her tight, wet heaven.

She makes me feel like a goddamn superhero. And if I could, I would stay right fucking here with her forever.

## CHAPTER ELEVEN

*Maeve*

Trying to take all of Wirth's abnormally long, thick cock is just as challenging as the first time. But once he's in, his big body moving inside of me and above me, the condom slick with my arousal, we fit together perfectly.

He's still being cautious, worried he'll hurt me when it's the exact opposite.

The hot, liquid pleasurable weight inside of my lower belly builds and builds until it bursts, making me tremble all over. It feels like I'm soaring and falling at the exact same time.

Wirth's arms wrap tightly around me to catch me, pinning me to the mattress with his weight as he growls out a curse next to my ear and his heavy body shudders against mine.

I love having him draped on top of me like an enormous, protective blanket. My fingernails trail up and down his back as we both catch our breath and the sweat on our skin begins to cool.

"Jesus," Wirth whispers, his lips pressing a kiss to my shoulder. "I thought I might have hurt you, but I think you killed me."

I laugh at his comment which makes my pussy squeeze around his shaft that's still inside of me, causing him to groan deep in his throat and shiver. Wirth isn't like other men after sex. He has to make an effort to pull out since he won't just slide free. He could stay inside of me all night if he wanted, and I don't think I would mind.

"This condom needs to go before it explodes," Wirth says when he starts to move off of me.

I grab his shoulders to stop him, worried he'll leave as soon as he stands up.

"Can you stay the night?" I ask him because I don't want to be alone. Talking to Rian earlier, bringing up the past that I've tried so hard to forget, makes me wish there was someone to hold me for a little while.

"Yeah, doll, I can stay," Wirth replies. Maybe I'm imagining it, but it sounds like he's hesitant.

"You don't have to..." I say since I want him to *want* to stay, not to do it out of some obligation he feels after sex.

"I want to," he replies, sitting back on his knees so I can see his face. And I think he's telling the truth.

"Good. I can make you breakfast in the morning," I offer.

"There's only one thing I want to eat for breakfast," he jokes with a grin as he swipes one long finger from my belly button down to my folds, making me squirm.

"That's fine too," I agree with a smile.

Wirth rolls out of bed to dispose of the condom in the bathroom and then strolls back into the bedroom confidently, like he could walk around naked all the time and not have any self-consciousness. And why should he when he looks that good?

Thankfully, he climbs into bed without putting his clothes back on and lays his arm across the pillow, inviting me over. I go, cuddling up to his chest, happy to be in his arms and out of my shitty memories even if it's only for tonight.

"I'm really glad you came over," I tell him as I let my fingertips trail over his chest.

"What had you upset?" Wirth asks as he holds me against his body.

"Just the past...my brother. He reminds me of our father, and that's not a good thing."

Wirth's big, muscular body goes still. He doesn't even breathe before he asks, "Your brother?"

"Yeah," I agree, and then my head lowers when he sighs heavily. "But enough about me. Tell me something about you."

"Not much to tell," he grumbles. "I grew up poor, started stealing cars before I could drive them. Now I run the shop."

"Auto repair shop?" I ask.

"Not exactly," he responds. "I can fix cars, but mostly I just take them apart and sell the pieces. Chop shops have more risks, but also more rewards than a regular repair business."

"Oh, so you steal cars?"

"It's not that big of a deal," Wirth mutters. "The only victim is the insurance companies since they cover the loss."

"What if someone can't afford car insurance?" I lift my head to ask him.

"Trust me – the kind of nice, expensive cars we deal with – if they can afford a fifty-thousand-dollar car, then they have insurance or they stole it first," he says, making me smile and shake my head before I lay it back down on his chest.

"And here I was thinking you were a good guy."

"Never claimed to be good," he says. "I just told you I would fix your car and not ask anything in return."

"Yet here we are in my bed," I point out.

"You called me, remember?" he chuckles. "And the first night, well, I just didn't want you to go upstairs with that giant. He looked like he could rip you in half."

"He's not as big as you," I tell him, letting my fingers reach down to wrap around his cock and enjoying the way my touch has him sucking in air.

"You're trying to kill me, doll," he grits out.

"I'm trying to make you feel good."

Wirth's fingers tighten in the back of my hair, lifting my face so he can lean down and kiss me. When he pulls away, he says, "You do that without touching me."

∽

## Wirth

AFTER AN AMAZING NIGHT with Maeve and an even better morning when I made good on my promise to have her for breakfast, I make myself leave her warm, strawberry and vanilla scented bed, intending to do more surveillance in the area before heading home – this time at the only Irish pub in town.

All I know is that I was fucking relieved when Maeve mentioned her brother. That must have been the man I saw yesterday. I'm a dick for thinking the worst.

"I had fun," I tell Maeve, leaning over to kiss her lips where she's still tangled up in the sheets, even though the words don't seem quite adequate enough.

"Me too," she says with a smile. "We should do it again sometime."

"Yeah, we should," I agree. But in the light of day, and without a heavy dick, it's a little easier for me to remember that I can't completely trust Maeve just yet. I need to try and keep myself from falling for her even more until I know for certain that she didn't have anything to do with the shooting at the Knights' bar. I also want to make certain she isn't fucking anyone else now that we're...doing whatever it is we're doing.

"Oh, and I've got my paint crew working on your car now. Hopefully it'll be ready in a few more days."

"That's great. Thank you. I don't have anywhere to go, so there's no rush."

"Good. I'll call when I know more," I tell her.

"Thanks, Wirth. Have a safe trip back," she says sweetly.

"Thanks," I reply before I finally force myself to walk away from her.

It's on the tip of my tongue to ask if she's going to see any other men, but I hold back. It's a little too soon for that conversation. Even if I don't want to think about her with another man, we've only had one night together. One and a half if you count our first time before shit went down at the bar. I have no right to be jealous of how she spends her time apart from me.

As soon as I'm on my bike with my full helmet on to cover my face, I take a trip to the Irish bar on the other side of town. Unfortunately, it becomes pretty obvious that there's an exit for it off the highway heading back to Carolina Beach, right before the one where I found Maeve changing her tire. There are a ton of other businesses on the same strip, so that's probably just a coincidence and I'm reading too much into it.

What's not a coincidence, however, is when I spot the same black sedan that I'm almost certain was at her apartment last night. My blood pressure skyrockets at the sight. I don't know who I'm more pissed at – Maeve or myself. I fucking knew a man was at her apartment and still I somehow ended up falling right back into bed with her. I'm not sure what would be worse — if it was a guy she was fucking or her brother with connections to the Irish who she would, of course, put before anyone else.

Either way, I'm so fucking pissed I can't even see straight. I park a block away, hiding my bike between two big trucks to watch the place through my binoculars for a little bit while I seethe and try to figure out what to do.

When a group of guys come walking out of the bar, I put away my binoculars to try and zoom in with my phone to take photos. They're mostly blurry blobs, but maybe the Knights will recognize one or more of them.

The men divide up into two groups. Some, including the man who definitely has an auburn tint to his hair, get into the black sedan. The others pile into a black Jeep before taking off. I consider following them, but worry that my single motorcycle could stand out. So instead, I make a call, which is probably not the best idea given my current temper.

As soon as Maeve answers sweetly, I snap at her, "Who's the fucking Irish ginger?"

"W-what?" she asks.

"Maybe you're fucking around with more than one, but I'm talking about the Irish asshole that I saw leaving your place last night before I came over," I elaborate.

"Wirth…please, let me explain…"

"Explain what? That you fucking betrayed the Knights and nearly got two of my friends killed?"

"I didn't know that was going to happen!" she exclaims.

"Goddammit, Maeve! So, you did know there was going to be a shootout? That's why you took me to your place, isn't it?"

"I didn't know anyone would get hurt! They were only supposed to fuck up the bikes!"

"What the hell did you think would happen when your friends shot up the place with people in it?" I yell at her.

"They're not my friends! I swear! Please, come over and just hear me out, Wirth. Please!"

Hearing her say my name, it does shit to me, not just my dick, but it squeezes my entire chest. But now that I know her true colors, I can't fall for her shit again.

"If you're smart, you'll pack your fucking bags and get out of town before every Dirty Ace in the country comes after you and burns down this town," I warn her before ending the call. When she calls again, I ignore it and block her phone number.

I'm so fucking done with her.

## CHAPTER TWELVE

*Maeve*

"Shit. Shit, shit, shit!" I yell when my second and then third call to Wirth won't go through. The first time I get his voice mail, but after that I simply get a message saying, "this customer is not available at this time." I think he blocked my fucking number! I throw the phone at the wall, hoping it breaks. Not only have I ruined things with him, but I've also put Rian in danger.

Wirth knows it was the Irish that shot up the Knights' bar. I'm not sure how he knows, but he does.

It was only a matter of time before the Dirty Aces and Knights figured it out. I had just hoped that I would have been able to convince Rian to leave by now.

Maybe there's still time to at least convince Wirth to postpone the revenge against the Irish. I have to at least try.

I run over and pick up my phone that surprisingly still works thanks to the protective case I have on it. My trembling hands pull up the number for Crystal, another club girl. She hasn't been very friendly to me, but I'm hoping a little cash will change her mind.

"Hello?" she, thankfully, answers.

"Crystal, hey, it's Maeve. I need to ask a huge favor."

"Maeve? Have you heard from the Knights? When are they coming back?"

"Ah, I'm not sure and I need to try to find them, so could I borrow your car? I'll pay you a grand for today and another grand tomorrow if I'm still using it."

"Two grand? Where did you get that kind of money?" she asks.

"Inheritance," I admit with a wince. "So, what do you say?"

"Yeah, sure. I'll bring it over now to the bar and have Wanda pick me up."

"Thank you," I tell her with an exhale of relief. "I owe you one. And you two shouldn't stay at the bar for long. No telling if the assholes who shot up the place will come back."

"No shit," she says. "I hope the Knights destroy whoever it was who did it."

"Uh-huh, me too," I lie. No matter how badly Rian fucks up, I would never wish death on my brother. Sometimes, I forget I'm his sister and not his mother since I practically raised him. Our father was always too busy to give a shit. The only reason he wanted a son was to brag about his heir. He didn't have any plans for changing diapers or sitting up all night with Rian when he was sick or teething.

I pack up a tote bag with my phone charger, wallet, a wad of cash, my phone, and a change of clothes. Not that I expect Wirth to let me stay with him now that he's figured out the truth; I just want to make sure I'm prepared.

I've just changed into a fresh pair of jeans and a tank top when Crystal texts me, saying she's at the bar.

I hurry out the door and down the street so she won't have to wait long in case Cormac decides to do another drive-by.

"Crystal, hey," I say as I walk up and find her standing near the side door beside her little beat-up car. I really hope it makes it to

Carolina Beach. If not, I'm guessing Wirth isn't likely to help fix another one for me. Hell, I may never see the car in his shop again. I would deserve nothing less than him chopping up my Honda and selling the parts.

"Here you go, girl," Crystal says, dropping her car keys into my palm. I pull out my roll of cash and count out two-thousand dollars in hundreds, then offer it to her. "Here."

"Thanks," she says with a grin as she folds up the bills and stuffs them in her purse. "Looks like the bar is still locked up tight." She nods to the building that now has boards over the door and windows. Guess the guys had someone come over and secure everything after they left. In red spray paint, someone wrote across one of the boards, "We're coming for you fuckers!"

They weren't called the Knights of Wrath for nothing, after all.

"Oh, there's Wanda," Crystal says, pointing to the red convertible that pulls up to the curb.

"Thank you again for this," I tell her.

She waves and says, "Just call when you're done, and we'll meet you here."

"Okay," I agree.

"Be careful!" she calls out before disappearing into the passenger seat.

I didn't think the other girls liked me, especially Crystal, but maybe the near-death experience from the other night has brought everyone closer.

If they found out that I knew what was going to happen, I would probably be beaten bloody by all of the catty girls, and again, I would deserve nothing less.

∼

*Wirth*

"You okay, man?" Malcolm asks when I show up at the pool hall, still fucking furious.

I look at the man who has been one of my best friends for years now, gauze covering the wound on his shoulder, and realize how close we were to losing him. If he hadn't dragged Naomi to the floor when he did, the bullet would've struck him in his head.

And Maeve knew what the Irish were going to do but did nothing to stop it. No, she was so unconcerned that she fucked me while it was happening.

Now I can't keep that shit to myself a second longer. I have proof – the man who was at Maeve's was with those assholes at the Irish pub.

"It was the Irish," I tell Malcolm. "They're the ones who shot up the Knights' bar."

Narrowing his eyes, he asks, "How can you be so sure?"

Shit. No matter how angry I am at Maeve, I still don't feel right dragging her into the middle of things. The guys will hurt her. They wouldn't normally touch a woman, but when she nearly cost three of them their lives and put more at risk – like Malcolm's woman, the mother of his child – they won't care about her gender.

So, I come up with another lie, one to protect her, for whatever reason.

"I was driving around last night and this morning and ended up in Wilmington," I admit.

"You shouldn't have gone alone," Malcolm grunts.

"I know, but I couldn't sleep, and there I was, outside the Irish pub. One of the cars had bullet holes in it and busted windows."

"No shit?" he says. "You're certain."

"I'm pretty damn sure it was the Irish."

He nods and then runs his fingers through the front of his long brown hair. "The Knights haven't been able to come up with any names of who else might've come after them. It had to have been the Irish."

"Yeah," I agree with a sigh.

"Did you see any of them?"

"A few. About eight came out of the pub. They got into two cars and left. That's when I came back here."

"Okay," Malcolm says. He rubs his bearded chin. "So, we know there are at least eight, but we should be prepared for double that number. I'll call in all the Dirty Aces chapters. If everyone shows up, we should have two dozen men. Think that's enough to take them on?"

"Ah, yeah, I mean I would hope so," I reply. Then I can't help but lower my voice and ask, "Are we sure it's worth the risk to our men to fight the Knights' battle for them?"

"Those men are wearing our patches now," Malcolm says. "They're one of us. Anyone comes for one, comes for all of us, right?"

"Right, yeah," I agree.

"Let's get everyone to the table. Now that Hunt's back, it's time to get to work."

"All right," I agree before I go round up Silas, Nash, and Devlin, who are playing a game of pool with Silas's girl, Cora. Her red hair stands out even more than usual tonight. Holy shit! What if she has ties to the Irish?

No, that's just my fucked-up head, trying to make shit up to take the blame off of Maeve.

Shaking those thoughts away, I tell the guys, "Malcolm's calling a meeting."

"Now?" Nash asks.

"Now."

"It's go time," Silas says, laying his pool stick down and giving his woman a quick kiss. "Be back as soon as I can."

"Okay," she agrees.

As we start walking to the chapel, I tell them, "We shouldn't leave Cora out here by herself."

"The prospect is outside," Devlin replies. "He'll let us know if anyone rides up."

"And we're sure we can trust him?" I ask.

"He's solid," Nash says. "I talked to him and had Lucy run his background." Leaning closer to whisper to me, he says, "She had already run backgrounds for the Knights. Everyone is clear."

"Good," I say, because that makes me feel a little bit better, which is ironic because if anyone is hiding shit, it's me.

## CHAPTER THIRTEEN

*Maeve*

Luckily, the Dirty Aces hangout isn't some secret. It's a pool hall that's in the middle of Carolina Beach with a long row of bikes parked out front. I wave to Freddy, the former Knights' prospect who is standing guard at the door, and then find a parking spot.

"Maeve? What are you doing here?" Freddy asks when I walk up to the door with Crystal's car keys in my hand.

"I need to talk to Wirth."

"Wirth?" he repeats, his brow creased in confusion. "Oh, one of the original Aces?"

"Yeah. Is he inside?" I ask.

"He is, but I think the guys all just went into the chapel for a meeting."

Shit. Right this second, they're probably talking about how and when they're going to hit back the Irish.

"I really need to talk to him," I say impatiently.

"You can go on inside. There's another old lady in there hanging out."

"Okay, thanks," I say, even though I'm not sure if I'm going to sit around and wait for Wirth.

After only hanging around a few weeks, I already know that in the MC world not even old ladies are supposed to interrupt a meeting, much less a club girl who the guys occasionally fuck.

I pull open the door that jingles before I go through it and find a beautiful redhead sitting on one of the bar stools alone, playing on her cell phone.

"Hi," she says.

"Hi. Everyone still in the meeting?" I ask.

"Yeah, it just started," she says. "Want to have a drink with me?"

"I really need to talk to Wirth."

"Oh. Well, I haven't been around here long, but I don't think it would be wise to interrupt, not today."

She's probably right. So, I reluctantly decide to wait, climbing up on one of the barstools next to her.

"I'm Cora," the woman says, offering me her hand.

"Maeve," I say as we shake.

"Maeve," Cora repeats. "That's Irish right? Doesn't it mean…intoxicating?"

"Ah, yeah. It is," I say, glad that no one else is around to hear that information.

"Mine is too, but Cora just means heart or maiden, so lame."

"So, you're Irish too, a natural redhead?"

"Yeah. And I've been hearing that's not a popular thing to be right now since it may have been the Irish that shot up the Knights' bar. I told Silas I should probably stay home, but he's so protective."

"Sounds like he's a good one."

"He is," she agrees with the dreamy smile of a woman in love.

Cora and I chit chat until the door to the meeting room finally opens.

I'm off my barstool in a heartbeat, hurrying over to look for Wirth.

"Maeve?" Hunt says in surprise when he comes out first. "What are you doing here? Worried about us so much you couldn't stay away?" he asks as he wraps me in a tight bear hug.

"That's right," I agree. "How are you?" I ask, noticing the gauze wrapped around his head and covering his ear.

"On the fucking mend," he says.

Right before he lets me go, I spot Wirth over his shoulder. He comes to a complete stop and stares at us.

"I'll catch up with you later," I say to Hunt before I go around him, saying hello to some of the other guys until I reach Wirth.

"What the fuck are you doing here?" he whispers under his breath.

"I needed to talk to you, and you blocked my phone calls," I tell him. "Please, Wirth?"

"Who's this? Who is she?" a big, tattooed man with shoulder-length brown hair asks when he strolls up next to Wirth.

"Malcolm, this is Maeve. Maeve, this is the president of the original Dirty Aces. He was almost killed the other night," Wirth grits out.

"Ah, it was just a scratch," Malcolm says with a pat to his wounded shoulder. "Now I understand why Wirth went MIA..." he trails off as he eyes me up and down with obvious male appreciation.

"Yeah, but would *Naomi*?" Wirth snaps at him.

"Oh, fuck off," Malcolm says before he chuckles and walks away.

"Can we talk?" I ask Wirth when the other man is out of earshot, nodding to the empty room behind him.

"I'm not letting you in there," he says, grabbing me by my elbow and pulling me toward the front door. He's muttering under his breath so no one can hear, but it sounds like he says, "For all I know, you'll plant a bug in it."

Outside and down past all the store fronts, Wirth finally comes to a stop and lets me go in the alley.

Glancing around, he says, "Huh, this reminds me of the alley where Fiasco was shot twice and nearly died."

"I swear I didn't know they were going to shoot anyone!" I tell him again.

"That's the biggest load of horseshit I've ever heard!" he yells back.

"It's the truth! Cormac told me they were going to do a drive-by to scare the Knights, to try and run them out of town, hit up the bikes."

"Do you honestly think those men inside would run from a few stray bullets?" Wirth asks.

"I-I don't know."

"Yes, you do! This is war, Maeve! You had to have known that, so save your lies for someone who will buy them!"

"I was just trying to protect my brother, okay?" I finally admit to him.

"Your brother. Right."

"His name is Rian, and he's only eighteen. He just turned eighteen, but now he thinks he's some bad ass soldier for the Irish. Cormac is in charge, but only for a few more years, until my brother is ready to take over and follow in our father's footsteps. He's all the family I have, and I can't lose him!" I tell him through the tears blurring my vision.

"So, let me see if I've got this straight – you were a goddamn plant in the Knights to get intel for the Irish, including when they were having a big party with everyone there?" Wirth asks.

"That's…yes, but it's not as bad as it sounds!"

"It's sounds really fucking bad, Maeve. There's no other way to spin it! You're a traitor, plain and simple. You fucked all the Knights and were giving information to their enemy!"

"I made a deal with Cormac. He said he needed my brother, and all of the guys who think Rian is supposed to eventually lead, to help him keep the Knights from taking over his drug business or whatever. I told him I would help try to get them to leave if he would figure out a way to push my brother out when the Knights are gone. I didn't want anyone to get hurt, I swear!"

"Well, three men did get hurt. More could have, including their women. Do you have any idea what they would've done if one of those guys lost their girl? They would've torched the entire earth to go after the people responsible, you included!"

"I know that!" I exclaim. "I'm sorry."

"Finally, you apologize," he grunts. "And the fucked-up thing is, I don't even know if you mean it."

"Of course I mean it! I'm not the horrible person you think I am."

"Could've fooled me. You acted like a bitch from the second we met."

"That…I told you I was sorry for that too," I tell him. "It's just, I haven't ever really been around many decent guys."

"And the first one you meet, you try and get his friends killed," he says through clenched teeth. "Do you have any idea how fucked I am for leaving with you? The Knights think I'm the traitor!"

"I'm sorry!" I say yet again, knowing it's too insignificant for what I did.

"Fine. You've apologized. You can leave now," Wirth says.

But I can't leave. Not yet.

When I don't say anything or move, he chuckles darkly. "Oh, I get it now. You think I would actually betray the fucking MC, my own fucking brothers, to help save yours after he helped shoot them up? You may be hot, but you're not that fucking hot."

"Please, Wirth. Rian is only eighteen! Do you remember being that age? Doing stupid shit without thinking?" I ask him. "I don't know how long you've been a member of the MC, but we grew up surrounded by violence. My father practically shoved a gun in Rian's hands before he could walk."

"That's not my problem," he replies, crossing his arms over his chest.

"No, it's not your problem. It's mine. I just thought…I thought you were a good guy, one who wouldn't like having the death of a stupid boy on your conscience."

"He apparently didn't mind having a death on his," Wirth points out before he lowers his arms and turns to start walking away from me. Without turning around, he calls out, "Get the fuck out of here, Maeve, before I tell everyone what you did!"

And I know then it's only a matter of time before I get a call or someone shows up at my door, telling me my brother is dead.

## CHAPTER FOURTEEN

*Wirth*

As soon I walk back into the pool hall, I go behind the bar, grab what's left of the Crown Royal we have on hand, and start chugging.

"Fighting with your old lady?" Devlin asks, leaning his forearms on the other side of the bar.

"I don't have an old lady," I assure him.

"That Maeve girl is pretty hot…" he trails off.

After I swallow a quarter of the bottle, I tell him, "Maeve was a fucking mistake that I'll regret for the rest of my life."

"Damn. That's harsh, bro," he says with a chuckle. "What the hell did she do to you?"

"Nothing."

"Nothing? She did nothing and you're over here drowning your liver in whiskey while badmouthing her?"

"Guess so," I tell him. "Shouldn't you be home with your woman before shit goes down tomorrow night?"

"Yeah, later. She took the Dickhead to some gamblers anonymous meeting. Like that's going to help him be less of a fucking tool."

"What dickhead?" I ask in confusion. "You don't mean her brother, do you? The one who knowingly pimped her out to a crime boss for a night?"

"The one and the same," Devlin says, yanking the bottle from my hand and taking a big gulp before slamming it on the table.

"I can't believe you let that shit fly."

"What am I supposed to do?" he asks. "Tell Jetta she can't be around her own brother because he might sell her out again? I can't make her choose between us. He's her family and I'm just her fiancé, for now. We can't pick our blood family, but we have to do our best to stand by them."

"I'm glad I don't have any siblings," I grumble.

"Me too," Devlin says.

"Maeve's brother is actually causing some…conflict," I admit to him without going into details.

"Oh yeah? You two only fucked once, and the family is already causing problems?" he jokes with a grin.

"Something like that."

"Don't make her choose between him or you. It won't end well," he says.

"I wasn't going to," I huff. "But, ah, she wants me to help him because he's young and stupid."

"How young?" Dev asks.

"Eighteen."

"That is still young," he agrees. "Dudes don't mature until we're, like, twenty-five or thirty."

"He's old enough to vote and serve in the military," I remark.

"Yeah, but probably not smart enough to make good decisions yet. If you like her, maybe you should give him a break."

"You don't know what that would mean…" I trail off, downing the rest of the whiskey.

"Then don't, I guess, if you never want to see her again."

"I don't want to see her again," I mutter.

"Bullshit," Dev says with a chuckle. "If you didn't care about her, we wouldn't be having this conversation. She wouldn't have you all worked up."

"It's complicated."

"Isn't it always when it comes to women?" he asks.

"They're not worth the fucking trouble."

"Eh, I would beg to differ, but unlike you, I've got a woman waiting in my bed for me every single night, ready to take on the day with me when the sun comes up, no matter what happens. There's no amount of trouble I wouldn't endure for Jetta."

"And that's what they call being pussy whipped," I say with a roll of my eyes at his sappy ass.

"That's what they call loving someone – sticking by them through the good and the bad, even if the bad is their fault."

I can't tell Devlin that it's not the same for me with Maeve. I barely know the woman. We fucked a few times and that was it. I don't owe her anything, and I certainly don't have any loyalty to her brother, who is the MC's enemy.

In fact, I think I need to remind myself what he did.

"I'm going to see Fiasco," I tell Devlin. "Tell the guys I'll see them later."

"Yeah, okay. Tell him we're thinking about him."

"I will," I agree before I head out on my bike. Thanks to the anger burning through my veins, I don't even feel the slightest buzz from the whiskey.

∼

*Maeve*

I CALL Rian as soon as I sit back down in Crystal's car.

"Yeah?" he answers.

"The MC is planning something. It won't be long before they come after the Irish."

"I've already told you that we'll be ready for them. We've got cameras everywhere around this joint."

I hear the loud hum of a group of motorcycles right before a group pulls up across the street.

"The MC is bringing in more guys, ones from out of town," I tell Rian. "You all will be outnumbered."

"Not a problem. In fact, we figured that would happen. We've got a shitload of guns and ammo waiting. But it would be better if you could find out exactly when they'll be here."

"I can't do that! They're not telling me anything else," I say, refusing to admit to him that Wirth knows I'm a traitor and also unwilling to help my brother hurt anyone else. "Leave while you still can, before everything goes to hell!"

"I can't leave Cormac," Rian says. "My job is to protect him."

"No, his job should be to protect you," I argue. "You're supposed to be the one they follow."

"Well, that's not how it works right now, and I'm done talking about this shit with you."

"You know as well as I do that Cormac deserves everything that happens to his sorry ass!"

"Don't fucking say that!" Rian snaps at me, sounding so defensive and unlike my little brother. "You don't know him like I do."

"No, I know him better. You're fucking blind and think everyone is as loyal as you are," I say with a roll of my eyes he can't see before I end the call.

My brother is too damn stubborn to admit when he's wrong or when Cormac is in the wrong, and that error in judgment is probably going to cost him his life.

## CHAPTER FIFTEEN

*Wirth*

"Hey, Joanna. Sorry to bother you," I say when the kind nurse opens her door later that night.

"No, you're fine," she says in a rush as she reaches up to redo her ponytail that's coming undone, her cheeks a little flushed. "And you came at the perfect time – he's actually awake and talking!"

"He is?" I say in surprise.

"Yeah. Finally, right?" she laughs nervously. "Come on in."

"Thanks," I say as I step into the house and go right to the bedroom.

When I walk in, Fiasco is sitting up, his torso bare other than the bandage on his side under his ribs. "Oh, it's just you," he says before he falls backward on the pillow again.

"Ah, just me? Thanks for that warm reception," I joke with a grin, glad to see him not only conscious but more alert than I expected.

"Sorry, that's not what I meant," he says just as Joanna comes in behind me.

"Would you like something to drink, Wirth? What about you, Phillip?" Joanna asks.

"Phillip?" I repeat in confusion. "Who the fuck is...oh."

All this time I've known Fiasco and I had no clue that his real name is Phillip. Seems odd he has such a normal name for such an unusual man. And really, to the guys in the MC, he'll always be Fiasco.

"I would love some water," Fiasco, aka Phillip, tells Joanna.

"I'm fine, thanks," I reply before she hurries out of the room.

"So, how are you feeling?" I ask him. "You look better."

"Yeah, yeah. I'm good," he says, watching the door intently before his wide brown eyes come back to me. "Wait. You're not here to take me home, are you?"

"Ah, I don't know. I wasn't even sure if you would be awake or not. Are you ready to go home?"

"Fuck no!" he exclaims. Lowering his voice, he says, "Did you see the hot piece of ass waiting on me?"

"She's a nurse," I remind him.

"She's a goddamn angel," he says with a sigh as his head falls back onto the headboard.

"Fine. But she's also Nash's sister, so don't even think about...well, about the things you normally think!"

"His sister?" Fiasco says, his jaw dropping. "I didn't know he had a sister."

Whispering, I go over to his side of the bed and tell him, "You still don't. You can't say a word! She doesn't know yet."

"Oh. Okay," he replies just as Joanna returns with a glass of water.

"Here you go," she says, coming to the side of the bed so that I have to step back out of the way. Then, she lifts the glass to Fiasco's lips and holds it while he sips like a helpless child. Jesus Christ, he's milking this for all it's worth.

"I brought you more pain killers too," Joanna says. Fiasco opens his mouth wide, and she places a pill on his tongue that he swallows with the sip of water she gives, followed by a second. "Now, I'll let you two have a little privacy."

"Thank you, angel," Fiasco tells her retreating back, probably her ass, before she disappears, watching her like a lovesick puppy. When she's gone, he says, "I never want to leave here."

"Oh, you're going to leave here, just as soon as Joanna says you're recovered enough," I tell him. "She's been taking time off of work after we busted in on her that night with three shooting victims."

"Three?" Fiasco asks. "Who else got shot?"

"Oh. Ah, Malcolm's shoulder got grazed, and Hunt, the president of the Knights, took one to the side of his head. Both are fine now."

"Do they know who it was? Who did the shooting?" he asks.

"Did you see anyone?"

"Ah, not that I remember. I had just finished coming for the second time. You know how it is after a release. I was floating high when I went down like I'd been, well, shot."

"We're pretty sure it was the Irish. They're not fans of the Knights showing up in the area and were trying to run them off."

"That was stupid," he says. "Like a few bullets would scare us away?"

"Yeah, stupid," I agree, scrubbing my palms over my face.

"So, what's the plan? Aces going to hit them back?"

"You know it," I reply. "Tomorrow morning before the sun comes up, when the bar is empty other than their own people."

"Light 'em up for me," Fiasco says, clutching his side with a wince.

"We will," I promise him. "Take care of yourself."

"I'm so fucking tired," he says. "Which is strange since Joanna said I have been sleeping all day."

"You're recovering from taking two bullets. Your body needs to heal."

"Yeah, she said some shit like that too," Fiasco mutters. "Pretty lucky she was around to help save me. I think I was going toward the light, man," he says.

"Well, I'm glad you stayed in the darkness," I tease him.

"I'd go to hell and back for Joanna," he says with a goofy grin.

"Watch yourself," I warn him. "If you don't, Nash might come after you with a gun."

"Yeah, okay," he agrees. "Will you ask her to come back in here on your way out?"

"Sure thing."

If the nurse's attention is what he needs to recover, then that's what he should get for now. I just hope he doesn't get too attached.

I find Joanna in the kitchen, leaning against the counter drinking what smells like coffee even though it's late. "He's asking for you," I tell her.

Sitting her mug down on the counter, she says, "I'll go right on in."

"Not sure how you ever get any rest with him demanding care and taking over your bed," I remark. "Just let us know when you're ready for him to leave."

"Will do," she says before she disappears into his room.

I leave and mount my bike, intending to go back home or to the shop to work until I get tired, but instead, I find myself driving to Wilmington.

It's stupid, and I don't even know why I'm going to sit outside Maeve's apartment.

Guess I want to torture myself a little more for giving in to her not once but twice.

The same black sedan is parked there in her apartment complex. It doesn't take long to see the redhead coming out of her apartment.

From across the parking lot, I can't see her face clearly, but I can hear her sobbing. "Please, Rian! Leave with me! Walk away from Cormac before he gets you killed! *Please!*"

Maeve drops to her knees on the concrete and it looks like her face is buried in her hands as she cries loudly. But her brother seems unfazed. He just walks away and gets into his car to drive off, ignoring the emotional pleas of his older sister, who is trying her best to save his life.

It's one of the saddest things I've ever witnessed.

In that moment, I can't help but feel sorry for her.

Like Jetta, Maeve loves her brother unconditionally, even though he's making horrible decisions. Still, no matter how stupid he's being, there's nothing he could ever do for her to stop trying to protect him.

My illogical fucking heart makes a decision that my head isn't totally on board with. But that doesn't seem to stop me from climbing off my bike and walking to her.

Maeve is still on the ground sobbing when I reach her.

Grabbing her shoulders, I start pulling her to her feet. "Come on. Let's get you inside," I tell her as I heft her up over my shoulder. Her body is limp; there's no fight left in her. I could be anyone picking her up and taking her away and she wouldn't care. All that matters to her is her brother.

Inside her apartment, I lock the door behind me and then lower her to the sofa, laying her down on it with her head at one end and her feet at the other. She curls into the fetal position, facing me as she continues to cry.

Kneeling down in front of her face, I brush her hair back and say, "Listen to me closely, Maeve. I'm only going to say this once."

Her glassy eyes finally blink open and look at me a second before she pulls the neck of her shirt up to dry her face. "W-Wirth? What are you doing here?" she asks, voice shaky.

"Tomorrow morning, four a.m., there won't be anything left of the Irish pub. Tell your brother. Call and come up with a reason for him to leave and come here. No one else! Do you hear me, Maeve? The rest of those assholes have to pay for what they did."

"T-tomorrow? At four a.m.?" she repeats, and I nod. "Oh my god! Thank you!" she exclaims as she throws her arms around my neck and squeezes with all the appreciation in her body. "Thank you," she repeats.

When Maeve pulls back, her lips brush against mine for an instant before I push her away and get to my feet.

"No. That's not happening again," I tell her. "In fact, I never want to fucking see you again."

I turn around to leave before my dick tries to disagree with my pronouncement.

"Wirth, wait!" Maeve calls out, and the bastard appendage twitches with interest just hearing her raspy voice say my name.

"We're fucking done," I say without looking at her. "You better not fuck me over on this shit either."

∼

*Maeve*

WATCHING Wirth walk away from me doesn't hurt as much as seeing Rian do it to me, but I still ache all over.

He didn't have to tell me the MC's plan. In fact, I can't believe he did. I know how loyal those guys are to each other and have no doubt that Wirth has never done anything to betray his brothers until now.

If they find out, he could be kicked out or even killed. The man is risking his life to help me, to help my brother, when I don't deserve it.

I wish there was some way to thank him, but now he doesn't want anything to do with me. That's fair, all things considered. But still, I can't help but envy and hate the future woman who will come into his life one day.

Drying my face, I sit up on the sofa and then get to my feet in search of my phone. When I find it in my bedroom on the nightstand charging, I pull it free, then sit down on the edge of the mattress intending to call Rian. First, I try to figure out what to say. Should I wait until three a.m. and make up some excuse for needing him to come over? What if he doesn't answer the phone or his phone dies? No, I can't take that chance.

So even though Wirth isn't going to be happy, I decide that it's worth it to not only keep him safe, but all of the guys on the Irish side and the MC side.

Rian, the asshole, doesn't answer my call the first time or the second, which only makes me even more confident that I'm doing the right thing.

Finally, on the third try, he picks up and says, "I'm not changing my mind about this, Maeve! I'm not leaving!"

"I know you won't leave! That's not why I'm calling," I say in a rush. "Don't hang up. I have information about when the Dirty Aces are going to retaliate. I'll give it to you if you promise to do just one thing for me."

"And how the hell do you know the specifics?" Rian asks, sounding skeptical. He's right. It doesn't matter who I was sleeping with, the men in the MC wouldn't ever tell me their plans in advance for this very reason – in case I'm a traitor.

"I-I just do. I've been in touch with some of the Knights and over-heard the details." I would never give him Wirth's name. For all I know, Cormac could use that against him somehow to turn the club against Wirth. "Promise me, on my life, that you'll agree to my one condition and I'll tell you."

"Fine. I agree. What do you know?"

"In the morning at four a.m. they're going to attack the pub." When he doesn't respond, I ask, "Did you hear me, Rian? You can't be there tomorrow at four a.m.!"

"All right. Got it. Four a.m. I'll let Cormac know," he says with a sigh like he's about to end the call.

"Wait! You can't tell him or anyone else. That's my condition, and you promised me!"

"Then what the fuck is the point of you telling me then? You know I'm not going to leave Cormac and the other guys there to get murdered in their sleep."

"You can still get everyone out of the building, as long as you don't tell them the reason so that they can stay on the outskirts of the bar to attack the Aces from behind! There has to be some excuse you use, right? Rian? You swore to agree to my condition on my life!" I remind him.

"I'm thinking!" he shouts. "I may have an idea. Cormac's been talking about wanting to do some stupid beach bonfire thing one night. I'll make sure it's tonight and that everyone is so drunk we crash on the dunes."

"You think you can convince Cormac to do that this late?"

"I think so, yeah," he agrees. "He owes our family…"

"Good. Then that's perfect!" I say with a heavy exhale of relief. "You swore on my life, so you better not back out. If you do, I could end up dead for telling you what I know."

"That doesn't make any sense..." he says.

"Well, it's true," I reply even if it's not exactly the truth. I don't think Wirth would kill me, but I'm not going to take the chance that he could get killed in an ambush after he caved and told me how to save Rian's life. If the other guys in the MC find out I was involved in betraying them the whole time I was in their clubhouse, well, I wouldn't put it past Hunt to take his revenge out on me personally.

"Call me when you're at the beach so I know that everyone is okay," I tell Rian.

"Fine, *mom*," he says it like it's an insult, when that's exactly how I see him. I've been like a mother to him since he was born, even though I was only six. I had to grow up incredibly fast, giving up most of my own childhood years. Our father left me no choice and then made sure there was nothing left of my innocence when I was sixteen.

No matter what Rian does, I won't ever stop loving him. I just wish he didn't do so much stupid shit that puts his life in danger...and now mine.

## CHAPTER SIXTEEN

*Wirth*

There are two dozen men squeezed into our pool hall in Carolina Beach by two a.m., putting on bulletproof vests and loading up on guns and ammo.

I don't like this plan, but I'll go along with it because that's what it means to be loyal to part of a brotherhood. We have each other's backs; and when it comes to it, we would take a bullet for each other.

Fiasco is still laid up in bed at Joanna's, not because he loves it there, but because now he's running a high fever. The infection isn't going away with the antibiotics, so she's going to try and get her hands on stronger ones. At least she hopes it's just an infection and not some sort of internal issue.

So, this morning, before the sun comes up, we're doing this for him. For Malcolm and Hunt too, who could've been killed. That kind of violent attack against the MC can't go unanswered even if it means risking our lives. If we didn't hit back, other clubs and groups could think we're weak and try to encroach on our territory across the state and up in Virginia where we've expanded.

"Everyone have the address for the old mall?" Malcolm asks. "That's where we'll park our bikes and then head to the pub on foot, so the bikes don't give us away."

Once everyone nods or voices their agreement, we saddle up and are rumbling down the highway in only a few minutes. I'm so lost in my own thoughts that I'm on auto pilot as I ride in our convoy, only snapping out of my dark thoughts once Malcolm, out in front of the rest of us, pulls into a parking lot. We file in behind him, killing our engines and then immediately dismounting. We're out on the edge of the mall's lot, well away from any security cameras, but we're still careful as we cross the road on foot towards the Irish pub.

All the lights are off, including the pub's neon signs out front. A few vehicles are in the lot, but otherwise it's a ghost town. It's almost too quiet out here. I start to mention that when Silas kicks in the front door. At the same time, I hear pounding coming from the back of the building, then everyone is running inside.

The front room is where the bar is located, along with a few tables and chairs, and several booths around the sides. It's also empty, so we head down the hallway where someone calls out, "Hold your fire! The place is empty!"

"Empty?" Malcolm repeats, stepping inside one of the rooms and flipping on the lights. It's a messy bedroom where someone sleeps, but not tonight.

Sure enough, all of the six smaller rooms are in the same state as well as an office and the storage rooms.

*Fuck.*

"Fuck!" Malcolm exclaims, echoing my sentiments.

I should've known Maeve couldn't do the one thing I fucking told her, which was to let her brother know the plan without anyone else finding out.

What the hell was she thinking? Doesn't she realize that now, more than before, the MC is going to know someone ran their mouth, that we have a rat? And eventually, someone will figure out that rat is me...

"Now what?" Devlin asks. "Should we still rig up the bomb?"

"No," Malcolm clips out. "Everyone out! Now!" he yells, pushing us toward the front door. "For all we know, this is a goddamn trap!"

Jesus. He's right. My heart starts racing, worried that, by feeling sorry for Maeve and running my mouth to help her brother, I'm going to get us all killed, myself included.

But once we make it outside and don't find an angry Irish mob waiting to blow us away, I can breathe a little easier.

"Back to the bikes!" Malcolm orders, and we all march back silent, lost in our own thoughts.

*Maeve*

I SIT up in bed to answer my phone the second it rings. I've been holding it and my breath until the clock clicked past four a.m.

"Rian? Are you okay?" I ask him in a rush.

"You were right," he says softly like he's whispering to avoid anyone overhearing him. "The security cameras just alerted Cormac to motion. There were more than a dozen of them. Looks like they didn't trash the place or even steal anything. I can't tell if Cormac is relieved we weren't there or suspicious of me for suggesting we head out tonight. Heh, fuck you very much for that, I suppose."

"I don't care," I tell him in relief. "I don't care what he thinks as long as you're alive. How could he be mad or suspicious when no one died?"

"Because it's quite a coincidence, Maeve. He's been going through everyone's phone..."

"Everyone but yours?" I ask.

"Oh, he looked at mine too. You're the only person I get calls from. He hasn't forgotten about how 'close' you were to the Knights."

"Whatever," I tell Rian. "He can put the blame on me all he wants or come after me, but I don't regret it. He's being an idiot, and it's going to get you and him both killed if he's not careful."

"I'm sure he would love to hear that," Rian mutters. "Gotta go. Talk to you tomorrow."

"Okay," I agree as he hangs up.

Now, I can finally snuggle back down into my bed and try to get some sleep knowing that my brother and Wirth are both safe tonight.

## CHAPTER SEVENTEEN

*Wirth*

"Someone in this room is a goddamn rat!" Malcolm roars while slamming his fists down on the wooden table. There's barely standing room in the chapel; but for whatever reason, I think that's how Malcolm wanted it, all of us crammed together while he goes off on us, trying to put pressure on the traitor.

"If so, then why weren't the Irish there to ambush us?" Hunt asks. "It doesn't make sense for them to not take advantage of the situation. Where the fuck were they, and why didn't they get us when we were vulnerable?"

"Hunt's right," Dev agrees. "It doesn't make sense."

"No, it doesn't," Malcolm says, looking pointedly at me like he already knows I'm to blame. "And we're not leaving this fucking room until someone talks. No one but the men in here knew our plan. No one!"

Maeve is going to get me killed. I've always said that women are not worth the trouble, and here I am, my head on the chopping block because she's got me pussy whipped after less than two nights with her.

No, this is worse than being pussy whipped.

She's got the fucking whip wrapped around my neck about to hang me with it.

"I know who the rat is," I speak up and say. The room goes so silent you could hear a pin drop.

"Well, let's hear it," Silas grumbles from where he's standing next to me, practically breathing down my neck.

"It's me. I'm the rat."

A few guys swear, others gasp.

"You dirty motherfucker!" Hunt shouts, and then he pulls out his gun to point it at me. "It's your fault I almost died!"

"That's your own goddamn fault, you stupid son of a bitch!" I yell back at him, pulling out my gun from the back of my waistband to aim it just as fast. "Maeve's brother is a part of the Irish fucking mafia, you blind idiot!"

His right hand holding the gun lowers. "Maeve?" he repeats. "No fucking way!"

"Do you really not vet your girls?" Malcolm asks, not looking all that surprised. Shaking his head, he says, "Blinded by the pussy. We've all been there."

"So, what are we going to do? Kill the bitch?" Silas asks from beside me. I ram my elbow into his face without even a second thought. Blood pours from his nose but that doesn't stop him from swinging his fist at my face.

"You son of bitch!" he roars while laying into me.

"Stop it right the fuck now!" Malcolm says when he and some of the other guys intervene to pull us apart. "Open the door and put all the guns the fuck down now! The lack of oxygen is making us all lose our damn minds."

Finally, some of the men escape the chapel, Malcolm encouraging everyone but the original Dirty Aces members and new Knights to leave.

He doesn't shut the door, though, making sure that they can listen if they want, proving he has nothing to hide and won't be giving me any special treatment just because I'm part of his crew.

"You told Maeve our plan?" Malcolm asks as I keep rubbing my aching jaw that feels displaced when I open my mouth.

"I only told her so that she could get her brother out of there. He's all the family she has left. She wasn't supposed to tell them all. Rian's only eighteen."

"Eighteen-year-old boys can fight for their country, so they won't be getting a free pass from me," Malcolm says when he lowers himself into his chair at the head of the table. "Was he one of the shooters?"

"Yes."

"Then he's man enough to pay the fucking consequences!"

"If the pub hadn't been empty, sure, yeah, we could've taken out a few, maybe even the ones responsible for the shooting. But we would've lost men too!" I point out. "So, to me, I guess it was worth the chance. I don't regret telling her, and I won't fucking apologize."

"He has to be punished for his fucking betrayal!" Hunt declares.

"So that's it, huh? You turning in your cut?" Malcolm asks.

"If that's what you tell me I have to do, then I guess I won't have a choice, will I?" I ask him.

"Not unless you're going to set shit right on your own."

"What does that mean?" I ask.

"You made this mess. Now you need to clean it up," Malcolm explains.

"I won't let you hurt Maeve," I tell him.

"That bitch is mine," Hunt says through clenched teeth while cracking his knuckles. It's good to see his gun is no longer in his hands, but there's only one thing for me to say to that.

"Over my cold, dead body."

"That can be arranged," Hunt replies and then reaches again for the gun in his shoulder harness. Malcolm is faster, pulling his out and shooting it about two inches over the man's head.

"What the actual fuck?" Hunt yells when he ducks down, his eyes wide in surprise, mouth gaping in disbelief.

"You touch that goddamn gun again and I'll blow your head off myself, Hunt," Malcolm warns him. "This is all your fucking fault for not telling us about the Irish before you patched in and for not keeping your girls in line."

"My fault?" Hunt scoffs as he straightens again.

"That's right," Malcolm agrees. "Glad you're starting to get it."

"This is all on him," Hunt says, pointing his finger at me.

"I didn't get anyone shot or killed," I respond. "Fiasco still isn't on his feet because of you. So, turn your fucking finger right the hell around."

That finally shuts him up. Hunt leans his back against the far wall and slips his hands into his pockets. The man is a hothead. I think he could make a decent president eventually; he just needs to take responsibility for shit.

"What the fuck were you thinking, man?" Malcolm asks me.

I consider his question for a moment before responding. "Probably the same thing you were thinking when you kept Naomi around even after you knew she was stealing from you."

Malcolm's jaw clenches in anger, but I'm not finished.

"Maybe I thought the same thing that Devlin was thinking when we had to go on a murder spree to save his girl."

Dev holds his palms up in surrender. "You got me there."

"Do I need to call out Nash and Silas too, or are you all getting the fucking point?"

"There's a difference. Maeve can't ever be trusted," Malcolm says. "She'll never choose you over her own brother."

"She didn't know the Irish were going to shoot up the bar that night! She thought they were only going to damage the bikes to try and scare the Knights away," I explain.

"Bullshit," Hunt huffs from where he's still holding up the wall.

"Was she naive? Hell yes," I tell them. "But she did it to try and protect her brother. I think we can all understand that on some level, right?"

"The Irish are still our enemy for drawing blood first," Malcolm says. "And with her brother part of them, she's still our enemy too."

"I know that," I reply. "But if you give me one more chance to clean this shit up like you said, I think I may be able to smooth things out."

"Oh yeah? And what if you fail?" Nash asks.

"Then you can take my cut and kill me if that's what the table votes to do."

# CHAPTER EIGHTEEN

*Maeve*

Even after Rian called last night saying he was safe, I knew the beef between the MC and the Irish wasn't even close to being finished. That's why I couldn't sleep a wink. In my mind, I kept trying to figure out a way to get both sides to back down and have come up empty.

I'm not sure if there's nothing to be done or…

When I hear someone knock on my door late that afternoon, I'm shocked speechless when I look out the peephole and see Wirth on the other side. A pair of aviator sunglasses cover his eyes, and the rest of him is, well, bigger, angrier and sexier than he has any right to look. Except…something is missing. He's not wearing his leather cut over his t-shirt, which is odd.

I didn't think I would ever see him again. In fact, his last words to me were that we were done. I wish he'd told me he was coming so I could've changed. Instead, I'm wearing a pair of ratty old boy short panties and thin tank top with no bra, but I don't think he'll care what I have on. He looks too pissed to even notice.

I quickly flip the locks and open the door to let him in. "Hey," I say, sounding out of breath from just seeing him again.

"You fucked me over," he grits out, face tense, making me wish I could see his eyes to see if there's any chance he'll ever forgive me.

"What I did…it was for the best," I reply, crossing my arms under my breasts defensively. "None of your friends died and none of the Irish did either!"

"No, they didn't, but my neck is on the line now. Everyone figured out it was me who told you about our plan. Do you know what the MC does to assholes who betray them?" he asks.

"H-how did they find out? Do they know what I did?"

"Hell yes they know what you did, that you were only fucking the Knights to give intel back to the Irish. Hunt wants you dead."

"Oh," I say as I try to swallow around the huge knot in my throat.

"Call your brother and tell him you need to leave town, or you won't live to see tomorrow," Wirth demands. This time I know there's no arguing with him.

I go and grab my phone from where I tossed it down on the sofa and quickly find Rian's name in my favorites. He thankfully answers on the first try. Instead of wasting time, I blurt everything out. "I need to leave town for a while. Right now. Tonight. The Knights know I'm a traitor and they want me dead."

"Fuck," Rian says with a sigh. "I'll pack and be over as soon as I can."

"Thank you," I tell him, even though I know that while he may leave with me now, finally giving me what I've wanted all along, he will eventually come back.

"I'm so sorry," I say to Wirth when I end the call and go to him. "About everything. Thank you for warning me before and now. I wish there was some way I could make it up to you."

"Oh, I'm sure you can think of something you can do to repay me," he says when his hands shoot out to grab the hair on either side of my face. He catches me so off guard that my phone falls from my hand

and hits the floor. Spinning us around, Wirth walks me backward until I'm pinned between him and the hard wall. With his lips brushing mine, he says, "One last favor for a dead man?"

Hearing that makes my blood turn cold. I didn't mean to put him in danger by protecting my brother.

"Come with us," I beg him, yanking his sunglasses off and tossing them down to see his deep blue eyes. "Please? I-I'll spend every day trying to repay you."

"Let's start with you repaying me right now and go from there," he says, his jaw tight, neither refusing nor agreeing to my offer.

I don't have a chance to say anything else after his pouty lips crash down on mine. His tongue forces its way inside of my mouth with so much force that the back of my head hits the wall. After that, I'm lost to the lust, the need for him. I think I would do anything this man asks. So, when his hands slip from my hair to my shoulders, pushing me down, I gladly go, knowing that getting his dick nice and slick with my mouth is more for my benefit than his before he attempts to ram that monster inside of me.

I don't waste any time undoing his belt and the fly of his jeans, shoving the denim down to his knees to free his cock that springs up long and hard, nearly slapping me in the face. Wrapping my fingers around the base of his shaft to hold it still, I close my eyes and get to work licking it up one side and down the other before my lips part to take him deep into my throat.

"Fuck, Maeve," Wirth groans above me. When I glance up, I see he's got one palm flattened against the wall while the other comes down to cup the back of my head to guide my movements. Instead of watching me, his eyes are closed, head thrown back in pleasure.

Unlike before, Wirth isn't gentle about showing me what he needs. But all too soon, he's pulling me to my feet and spinning me around so that I'm facing the wall. I try to catch my breath while he tugs my boy shorts down. When his palm lands with a loud smack on my ass, I jump forward until the side of my face is flattened to the wall. My ass cheek is still stinging when Wirth pulls my hips back and then shoves his cock all the way into my pussy with one hard thrust.

"Oh god!" I scream at the intrusion. He's nearly the size of a fucking baseball bat. If I wasn't so accustomed to rough treatment, I would probably be sore afterward. But my body has learned to be accommodating, and I'm so wet for Wirth it doesn't hurt. I just want more – more of him and more of us together. "Please!" I beg when he doesn't move. He just stands there, filling me up with so much of him I can't breathe.

He finally does what I asked. His fingers dig into my hip bones even harder, then he pulls his cock almost all the way out of me before slamming in hard again, deeper than anyone has ever gone before.

"What the fuck are you doing to me?" Wirth pants against my ear in a rush, his entire body weight pressing me into the wall so that my nose is close enough to smell the paint. "Even when it's life and death, I would rather have you one last time."

"Me too," I agree on a near sob because I feel the same. I shouldn't want him, but this doesn't feel like a choice. Wirth is a necessity that I don't want to live without.

One of his hands comes around to squeeze my breast before getting frustrated by the tank top still covering it. His strong hands rip it right down from the neck so that it's gaping open. Squeezing my left tit, he presses his entire arm tightly to my chest, thrusting into me so hard and fast that I end up on my tiptoes. I wouldn't be surprised if there's an imprint of the front of my body being left on the wall.

My pussy clenches around his girth, pulling him impossibly deeper as my arousal coats his hot, velvety shaft.

Oh shit!

He's not wearing a condom.

That thought shouldn't make me come, but it almost sends me over the edge. Wirth isn't the type of man to be so careless. I love that he's so out of control with need for me that he didn't stop to put on a condom, like I'm not the only one lost to the lust.

As my inner walls begin to pulse around Wirth's pumping dick, trying to hold it inside of me, he says, "Oh fuck!" like he just realized the same mistake. I'm still riding him and the waves of pleasure when he abruptly pulls out, making me whimper at the enormous loss because I wasn't done yet!

Understanding my dilemma, Wirth strokes himself between my legs, pressing his length against my clit to keep getting me off while his hot, thick release lands on the wall before he shoves himself between my tight ass cheeks to finish coming there.

When the heat of his body leaves me, I look over my shoulder and find him stumbling backward before he slumps down on the sofa, his dick still hanging free from his pants. "That…wasn't part of the plan," he says out of breath.

"It wasn't?" I ask. "Because I liked it," I say when I pull my bottoms up and shrug out of my ripped tank to go to him. Kneeling between his legs, I ask, "What was the plan? To yell at me and tell me to leave?" Before Wirth can answer, I lean forward to take his semi-hard cock into my mouth to clean it off, loving his taste and mine combined.

"What are you doing?" he asks, now watching me suck and lick his dick unlike earlier.

"Worshipping you on my knees," I reply between licks. "You should get used to it."

"Yeah?" he asks, gasping loudly when I suck on his head.

Releasing him from my mouth, I say, "Tell me to stay down here on my knees for you the rest of my life and I would do it."

"I wish you could, doll," Wirth says just as there's a knock on my door.

In the afterglow haze, it takes me a few minutes to remember that Rian was on his way over.

"Shit," I say, slapping my arm over my bare breasts and looking around me for something to cover them.

"Go get dressed. I'll answer the door," Wirth tells me. "Time for me and your brother to finally meet."

"Okay," I agree as I use his knees to pull myself up to my feet. On the way to the bedroom, I hear his zipper go up and then he's opening the door.

## CHAPTER NINETEEN

*Wirth*

Maeve's brother staggers back two steps when he sees me answering the door instead of his sister. From far away, he looked like any other guy, but up close it's easier to see the youthfulness in his baby face. Thankfully, I'm also about three or four inches taller than him and have at least fifty pounds on him, which helps a lot for what I have planned.

"Who the fuck are you?" he asks.

"Maeve's friend," I tell him.

He looks me up and down, trying to decide if he should trust me or not. If I had been wearing my cut, I'm certain he wouldn't have.

"Where's Maeve?" he asks in concern.

"Changing."

"I'll be right out!" she calls from the bedroom, which is when her brother's shoulders finally relax, and he takes the steps to come inside.

I quickly shut the door and then attack him from behind, catching him off-guard. Grabbing his arms, I tug his wrists to his lower back while using my body weight to pin him face first to the wall in almost the exact spot where I just fucked his sister. He never saw it coming.

"What the hell?" he asks, trying to buck me off while I pull the zip ties from my pocket to try and get them on him as fast as possible. He pushes me back and away before I can fasten the damn things, so I have no choice but to take him to the ground and use my knees on his back to hold him down while I finally secure his wrists.

"Wirth!" Maeve shouts when she comes in and finds me on top of her brother. "What the hell are you doing? Get off of him!" she yells, trying to grab my arm to pull me up. I let her since I'm finished, going to stand in front of the door in case Rian's able to get to his feet and make a run for it.

"Sorry, doll," I tell her. "It had to be done."

"I don't...what are you talking about?" she asks while I pull my phone from my pocket and send the text I had already typed out before I came over.

"Your brother needs to pay for his mistake," I explain. "You can't protect him anymore."

"W-what?" she exclaims, covering her gaping mouth. "No. Please, Wirth! We can all three leave together!"

"It's too late," I tell her just as her apartment door opens. Malcolm and the guys come in to collect her brother. They got here quickly since they were around the back of the building just waiting for my text.

"No! Don't hurt him! Please! I'm begging you!" Maeve says as tears stream down her face.

"Smells like sex in here," Devlin remarks, wrinkling his nose. Malcolm looks at me and arches an eyebrow in question as Silas and Nash get Rian up off the floor.

"I did what I needed to do," I say in my defense, which I know is weak as fuck. "Shut up and take her too," I instruct them before Malcolm can comment. I know I'm too weak to do it. If she's left here, I have no doubt she would run to the Irish to tell them. If this plan of mine is going to work, then I need those Irish fuckers to be blindsided.

Maeve's pleading turns to anger after the guys zip tie her hands behind her back. "I can't believe you would do this to me!" she yells. "I hate you! I fucking hate you for this, Wirth!"

"Let's go, sweetheart," Devlin says as he grabs her elbow and escorts a sobbing Maeve out of the apartment.

"You fucked her first?" Malcolm asks when she's gone.

"Yeah, I did," I respond.

"I'll fucking kill you!" Rian yells as he gets dragged out by Nash and Silas.

"Pretty messed up," Malcolm says. "She'll never forgive you."

I turn away and start for the door, so he doesn't see me wince. "I had to figure out a way to distract her until he got here," I lie.

"Whatever you say, man," Malcolm mutters, shutting the apartment door behind him.

The guys get everyone loaded up in the stolen SUV we haven't chopped up yet, and I climb on my bike, glad I don't have to be in that vehicle with Maeve on the way back to Carolina Beach.

Instead of going to the clubhouse, we take them to Malcolm's old beach cottage, not the house he shares with Naomi and his kid.

The guys bring Maeve and Rian in. They take her to the bedroom and sit her brother down in one of the kitchen chairs, his arms around the back rails to keep him from going anywhere fast.

"How's the shoulder?" Rian asks Malcolm with a smirk, which was the wrong fucking thing to say. The kid has balls, but they're going to get him killed before I have a chance to fix what I fucked up.

Our president hauls back and knocks the shit out of the boy's face, sending a spray of blood across the wall. I can't help but be glad that Maeve is locked in the bedroom and didn't see it.

"Tell us about the Irish and maybe we'll let you live after you tried to assassinate me and fucking missed."

"Not gonna happen," the kid responds.

"Well, if you don't want to talk, maybe we'll knock your sister around a little until you change your mind," Malcolm says while I glare at him. I'm pretty sure he's bluffing, but I don't even like the threat of him hitting Maeve.

Rian doesn't say another word for the next half hour despite Malcolm's fists continuing to abuse his baby face.

Unable to take anymore, I decide to go check on Maeve.

In the locked bedroom, she's sitting on the floor with her back to the foot of the bed.

"Lean up, and I'll cut off your zip ties," I shut the door behind me and tell her. There is no risk in untying her. The windows have been sealed shut, and the door will be locked whenever someone's not in here with her.

She scoots forward without looking at me. Taking out my knife, I slice through the plastic and then hurry to put the knife away before she gets any ideas, like stabbing me in the chest with it for betraying her. Now she knows how I feel.

"He'll never talk," she mutters, wrapping her arms around her raised knees that are drawn up to her chest. "Rian would die before turning on Cormac."

"Guess we'll see. All we want is to know what his fucking problem is with the MC. Malcolm's threatening to hurt you, so he might just break before you expect."

∽

*Maeve*

I'M SO furious that everything in front of me is blurry from the anger and tears.

I thought Wirth cared about me the same way I cared for him. I thought he was going to leave with me and Rian so that we could be together and be safe away from the Irish and the MC.

I've never been more wrong about a man.

That's what I get for trusting one. I knew better. My own father showed me everything there was to know about men – they don't care about anyone but themselves. The one thing I never understood about our father was that he had plenty of money. Tons of it. So, did he just want to hurt me by taking my innocence from me? It's not like he needed the ten grand he made to feed us or keep a roof over our head. I told myself at the time that he must have been desperate for the cash; that's the only reason a father would hurt his only daughter so brutally. But when he died, I had all the proof I needed that he had millions in the bank, even back then.

"I'm sorry it came to this," Wirth says, making me scoff at his insincere apology as he towers above me in the bedroom. "I am," he says again. "And I'm sorry that I took advantage of you earlier…"

"Right," I huff. "You're just like every other man," I tell him. "All you wanted was one thing from me, like you think I'm nothing but a few body parts, not an actual person with fucking feelings!"

"You know that's not true," he replies. "I risked my fucking life for you and for what? You choose your brother over me, and I can't blame you. But don't act like you're the one who got fucked over."

I hate that he's right.

Even more, I hate that we met because of my deceit with the Knights.

I think I could've loved Wirth and he could've loved me if things had been different.

But they're not.

And now I don't know what the hell happens next.

## CHAPTER TWENTY

*Wirth*

Malcolm is only aware of part of my plans to set shit right. If I had told him what else I planned to do, he would've stopped me and called me a fucking fool.

And he probably would've been right.

I told him I needed to get out of the house for a while, to get some air.

Then I got on my bike and drove it right back to Wilmington.

When I park outside of the Irish pub, I lift the seat on my motorcycle and hide my gun in the storage compartment with my cut. For one reason or another, Malcolm hasn't demanded it back just yet. As I stand outside the bar, even I can admit I'm having second thoughts about this risky plan of mine.

All I know is that going in guns blazing is not going to make things better but worse with the Irish. So, I'm taking a chance.

A huge chance.

But that's how much I already care about Maeve, even though I shouldn't.

I open the front door and walk inside like any other customer. There are only five or six patrons sitting and drinking in the booths, at a table, or at the bar.

"What can I get ya?" the middle-aged, tall and lanky bartender asks me.

"I need to see Cormac."

"Did he know you were coming?" he asks.

"No."

"Then I doubt he's going to want to see you."

"Maybe if you tell him I know where one of his men is being held against his will, he'll change his mind," I reply, making his sunken eyes widen. I would never give up the actual location, but I knew that information would get his attention.

"I'll, ah, be right back," he says in a rush, tossing down his towel as he leaves the bar. He goes down the hallway where I know from before that the bedrooms are located.

There are two big men standing guard outside one of the doors. I'm guessing Cormac is hanging out inside. The bartender passes on my message to the men, and then one of them leaves to step into the room, then quickly returns, walking over to me at the bar.

"We'll need to check you for weapons," he announces.

"Check away," I say when I stand up holding my arms out to the sides. The guard pats me down thoroughly before stepping aside and nodding his chin for me to go into the room where he left the door open.

Inside is a man in his early to mid-thirties standing behind a desk. His hair is red and he's wearing a business suit with a vest, minus the jacket. I'm guessing he's Cormac, the one in charge.

"Who has my man?" he asks. "How the fuck do I know you're not lying?"

"Well, have you been missing anyone since last night? Perhaps another ginger? I'd say he's about eighteen and goes by the name Rian."

"Rian?" he whispers the name as he sinks down as if to sit and has to grab onto the desk when he realizes his ass is nowhere near the chair.

Interesting….

He's not reacting the way Malcolm would react to one of his guys being kidnapped, cool, calm and composed, possibly furious. Instead, Cormac looks distraught, like it's a close family member. Maybe the Irish have tighter bonds than the MC, which I find hard to believe. I watch his face as several emotions pass over it, giving him a minute to let everything sink in. When it finally does, the ginger goes from concern to anger in a heartbeat as he stands up straighter and pulls a gun on me.

I'm really getting sick and tired of people threatening me.

"Tell me where the fuck he is and who has him or I'll kill you right here!" he grits out between his clenched teeth.

I'm not scared of him. I think Hunt was probably more likely to pull the trigger than this man. "If you kill me, then you may never figure out the answers to your questions."

That realization has him slamming his gun down on the desk. "What the fuck do you want? Cash? Is this some kind of extortion?" he asks.

"I don't want your money. All I want is to work out a truce with you."

"A truce?" he repeats. "With whom? I didn't know we were at war with anyone."

"Cut the shit," I tell him. "We know it was you who shot up the Knights' bar the other night. You nearly killed three of our men, and now we have one of yours. If you don't stop lying out your ass, then we'll wipe you all out by the end of the week!"

"You'd like to think so," he grumbles.

"I know so." I don't know shit, but I can pretend I do. Most likely, the Dirty Aces do have more men since we called in all of our chapters.

"So, what would this truce of yours mean for the Irish?"

"It would mean you would leave the former Knights of Wrath,

now the Dirty Aces, the fuck alone. They're not leaving town no matter how badly you want them to."

"Then we still have a problem," Cormac says.

"Yeah, *you* have a problem. Your guy Rian's life is hanging by a thread, and your entire crew is about to become extinct. Looks like you're going to do whatever the hell I say, doesn't it?"

His dark green eyes blaze with anger. "If I don't get rid of the Knights or Aces or whatever the fuck they are now, then there won't be anything left of the Irish once they take all of our business away from us!"

"What business? Because I don't see the problem with having two places to drink when they're not even in the same block. You guys are across town from each other."

"Not the bar!" he exclaims. "Heroin."

"Heroin?" I repeat in surprise. "Jesus Christ. This has all been about heroin?"

"Yes."

"Then you're a fucking idiot," I tell him, causing his jaw to tick. "If you had just asked, we would've told you that the Knights are getting out of heroin after it killed their old president. It was a condition for us to patch them over to Aces!"

"Bullshit," he says, eyes narrowed in disbelief.

"It's the truth! We don't deal in that shit. The only thing we touch is weed and speed."

"That's all?" he says. "Just weed and speed, even in Wilmington?"

"In all of our chapters, so yes, that includes Wilmington now."

"Then I guess that solves our...rift with the Knights, once you give me my man back," he declares.

"Not so fast. You drew blood from three of our men. One is permanently maimed with a missing ear, one took a shot to the shoulder, and the other got shot twice and still isn't on his feet yet. We'll be lucky if he doesn't die from infection!"

Lowering his eyes to the paperwork on his desk, he nods and says, "So you want blood for blood?"

"That's the only thing that will calm down the former Knights and the rest of the Aces."

"And that blood is going to cost Rian his life?"

"Not necessarily," I tell him, hoping that Rian is still alive and none of the guys have put a bullet through his head yet. If so, this is all for nothing. There will probably still be a war with the Irish. And Maeve, well, I don't think she would ever recover from losing her brother. "How about we let you decide?"

"I get to decide who *you* get to kill?" he grits out.

"I didn't say anyone had to die. I said blood is owed for blood. That's the only way to even the score. It's not like I'm asking for three of your men to make up for the three of ours you shot."

"Just one?"

"If you'll agree to one man taking a bullet from the president of the original Dirty Aces, then I think I could convince them to back off and let Rian go alive."

"*You think*? Do they even know you're here? Who the fuck are you?"

"I'm Wirth Wright, one of the original Aces. If you agree, I'll try like hell to convince them to honor the truce. Otherwise, I wouldn't have come here alone risking my own life."

He pulls his chair up to the desk and takes a seat in it. "Then I guess I don't have much of a choice, do I?"

"Nope."

With a heavy sigh, he sticks out his arm for me to shake his hand. When I walk over to take it, he says, "I give you my word. We'll leave the Knights alone if they do the same and return our man in exchange for me taking one bullet."

"You're gonna take it?" I say in surprise as I drop his hand. "What if you die?"

"The truth is, I'm just filling in for Rian," he admits. "His family has led our people in the states for decades. After his father died, I took over until Rian was old enough to learn the ropes."

"You think he's old enough now?"

"Guess he'll have to be, won't he?" Cormac asks.

I'm not sure how Maeve will feel about that. Is that the reason she was trying to convince her brother to leave, not just to avoid getting caught in the crossfire but so that he wouldn't have to be in charge? At least if he's leading, he'll have men protecting him rather than be a grunt.

"If the pub's number is listed, I'll call your bartender out front when I know more," I tell him, and he nods his head in agreement.

"Hurry up!" he shouts when I start to leave. And I don't think he said it to be a dick but because he's honestly worried they could kill Rian.

I am too, which is why I hop on my bike and ride to Malcolm's old house as fast as I can possibly go while making sure the Irish aren't following me.

## CHAPTER TWENTY-ONE

*Maeve*

After trying to find a way out of the bedroom and realizing the windows weren't going to open and that there's nothing in the room to break them with, I give up and lay down on the bed.

I'm trying my best to not think about what the men are doing to Rian, what Wirth could be doing to Rian, even though I can hear the occasional thump and strangled curse.

A few stray tears drip down over my nose and hit the bedding when I think about how stupid I was to trust him. He told me to call Rian to come over before he touched me. He had a plan that whole time he was kissing me and inside of me. I don't think anyone has ever hurt me so badly. Well, at least not anyone that wasn't a relative. My father and Rian damaged me enough. That's why I've never been in a serious relationship with a man, because I know it would end with having my heart broken. And while Wirth and I weren't even close to being together as a couple, I thought he cared about me enough to not manipulate me or go after my brother.

When the bedroom door handle jiggles like someone's on the other side unlocking it, I pop right up into a sitting position, waiting to see who it is.

I wasn't expecting Hunt, although I guess I should have.

It's only the second time I've seen him since the night the bar was attacked. The side of his face is still red and raw with a bandage over his ear. That's all the time I have to assess him before he shuts the door behind him and then he's on me. His fingers wrap around my throat and squeeze, pulling me off the bed. I struggle to get my feet on the floor before I pass out from a lack of oxygen.

His eyes are dark and empty when he says, "If it were up to me, you and your brother would both be dead already. Nothing is worse than being betrayed by a goddamn whore!"

Even though his hand is hurting my throat, making me gasp, I'm relieved to know Rian is still alive after all.

The edges of my vision are starting to go black when Hunt finally releases me. I fall to my knees, thankful he let me go and didn't kill me yet. My fingers try and smooth the ache on the outside of my neck, and I have to clear my throat a few times before I can finally speak. "I'm sorry," I tell him honestly. "You do…what you have to…for family."

Grabbing my chin roughly between his finger and thumb, he forces my head back to look up at him. "Exactly," Hunt says. "Which is why you're lucky to still be breathing."

From the look on his face, I can tell he's still not convinced he shouldn't end me right here and now. But thankfully, the bedroom door opens and the pretty guy with jet black hair is filling it.

"Let her go," he orders Hunt. The furious man releases my chin but then his palm hauls back and slaps the shit out of the side of my face. "Enough, Hunt! Let's go. Wirth's called a meeting."

Just hearing his name stings more than my burning cheek.

"Coming," Hunt says, finally turning away and leaving me on the floor to stomp past the guy holding the door open.

"You okay?" he asks, his voice and his handsome face sounding sincere.

"Yeah. I'm just fucking awesome," I tell him sarcastically when I grab the side of the bed to pull myself up to my feet.

"Stay here. I don't think it'll be much longer," he says before leaving. I hear the lock turn from the outside, and then I'm a lonely, miserable prisoner again.

∽

Wirth

"WHAT THE FUCK was Hunt doing in there with Maeve?" I go ask Devlin in a frantic rush.

"She's fine. He just slapped her around a little," he says. "Nothing she didn't deserve."

That's easy for him to say. I wonder what he would think about an angry man being alone with Jetta.

Except, Jetta would never be a traitor to the MC or betray Devlin.

*Fuck.* Nothing is ever simple.

"What's going on, man?" Malcolm asks when everyone is gathered in the kitchen – all the original Aces, except for Fiasco, and the old Knights.

Maeve will have to wait. Right now, I need to convince ten men to put aside their pride and egos to prevent going to war with the Irish.

"I've worked out a truce with Cormac, the guy leading the Irish," I explain.

"You did what now?" Malcolm exclaims.

"I went and talked to him, trying to figure out what his problem was," I say, noticing that Rian, who is still seated in a kitchen chair in the middle of the floor with a swollen lip and eye but is otherwise no worse for wear, suddenly looks very interested in our conversation.

"Are you fucking insane?" Nash asks me. "You could've been killed!"

"I went in unarmed to talk, that's it," I assure them, and Rian seems the most relieved. "Apparently the Irish were under the impression that the Knights were still dealing heroin. They were concerned about the competition. I assured them that the Knights gave up heroin as part of their agreement to join the Dirty Aces. That is true, isn't it?" I ask Hunt.

"Well, ah," he rubs the back of his neck. "We're still…transitioning."

"What the fuck do you mean you're 'transitioning'?" Malcolm turns on him to ask. "We had an agreement."

"We haven't sold any in Wilmington," Hunt says. "We're just unloading the rest of our supply back in Fayetteville."

"I don't care if you have to flush it down the toilet. I want that shit gone today!" Malcolm shouts at him. "Either it goes, or you go."

"Fine, fine," Hunt agrees. "I'll make a call, and it'll be done."

"Good," I say. "And that means there's only one other thing left to deal with."

"What's that?" Silas asks.

"Cormac's agreed to make amends for the shooting by taking a bullet himself," I explain.

"What? No!" Rian yells. "He can't do that! Shoot me instead!"

Malcolm and the guys look from the boy to me with their brows raised in question. "Cormac was pretty adamant that he wanted it to be him and not Rian."

"That's ridiculous! He's in charge. He can't do this!" Rian declares.

"He said you were actually supposed to be the man in charge, once you decide to be a man," I tell him and the others.

"I'm not ready!" Rian says.

"Obviously," Malcolm mutters to him before turning his attention back to me. "So that's it. The Knights give up heroin, Cormac takes a bullet, and all is well in Wilmington?"

"That's it," I agree.

"Huh," Dev says. "If it was that fucking easy, why didn't the Irish just talk to us before?"

"That's what I said," I reply. "Guess they assumed the worst. From what I gather, they had an antagonistic relationship with the Knights."

"I still can't believe you went alone to negotiate," Nash says with a shake of his head. "You've got balls of steel, man."

"And I'm guessing he's also got a dick of steel if he's willing to go to all this trouble for a woman," Malcolm says with a chuckle. "She nearly got us all killed!"

"I know," I tell him. "But so did these assholes, and you voted to let them in." I point to Hunt and his crew.

"Touché," Malcolm replies. "So, when do we meet?"

"Tonight at seven at the pier?" I suggest. "There are no cameras and shouldn't be much of a crowd."

"Set it up," Malcolm agrees.

"Take me with you!" Rian begs. "I'll change Cormac's mind."

"What are we going to do with our captives?" Dev asks.

"Leave them here with you and Silas until the deal is done?" I offer.

"You good with that, Dev? Silas?" Malcolm asks the two men.

"Yeah," Devlin agrees.

"Sure thing, prez," Silas says. "As long as you take at least one of the other chapters with you to have your back."

"Will do," Malcolm agrees. To Silas, he tips his chin toward Rian and says, "Now that we're done with him, you can lock him in the bedroom with his sister."

"Will do," Silas responds.

"You coming with me?" our president asks.

"Hell yes. I set this up, so I want to be there to make sure it goes off without a hitch," I tell him.

"Good. Now I've got a few hours to decide where to shoot the bastard."

"Please don't! Take me!" Rian pleads as Silas and Dev pick up his chair and carry it and him to the bedroom.

"What's that about?" Malcolm whispers.

"I have no idea," I tell him as I watch the men disappear into the room and try to get a glimpse of Maeve. I know she doesn't want to see me, and I fucking hate it.

## CHAPTER TWENTY-TWO

*Maeve*

"Rian! You're okay!" I say when I shoot off the bed to go see him. Two men slam the chair he's attached to down and then leave, quickly closing the door behind them.

My brother's face is pretty messed up, but he's alive and can recover from a few superficial wounds. What worries me is that he's also distraught. His eyes are glassy, and it looks like he's hurting. Maybe the pain is worse than it looks. He could have some internal injuries.

"What's wrong?" I ask when I kneel in front of him. "Are you in a lot of pain?"

"We need to leave! We can't let them…" he chokes up, throwing his head back like he's trying to find the words.

"Can't let them what?" I ask. "Did they…are they going to kill you?" I ask as an invisible rope seems to tighten around my throat, right where Hunt's hands were squeezing before.

"No, not me! Cormac!" Rian shouts.

"Cormac? How did he get involved?"

"One of the bikers, the guy who answered your door, went and worked out a truce with him earlier."

"Wirth worked out a truce?" I say in surprise.

"Cormac agreed to it, but he's going to take a bullet from them to even the score! Why the fuck would he do that? Why can't it be me or anyone else?"

"I-I don't know," I reply as I try to figure out what this all means. "So, you're safe?" I say to be sure I have it right.

"Yes," he whispers, his head now hanging. "But Cormac..." he chokes up and can't finish his sentence.

Did Wirth work all of this out to save Rian? That doesn't make any sense since he's the one who had him dragged here in zip ties! He was probably just trying to avoid any more bloodshed from his friends, the other bikers. God, I really wish I knew what was going on out there!

"I love him, Maeve."

It takes several seconds for Rian's random words to sink in because I'm so lost in my own head.

"Who do you love? Cormac?"

"Yes."

"Oh, I know you do. He's been like a father..." I start but Rian shakes his head and interrupts.

"No, Maeve. I'm *in* love with him."

*I'm in love with him.*

Those are the last five words I expected to hear from my brother's mouth because he's so young and inexperienced...

"Oh," I mutter and then slap my palm over my still gaping mouth in understanding. "You and Cormac have...you're..."

"Gay." Rian's eyes are closed tight as if it's so painful to say the word that he can't look at me while speaking it. "I've never admitted that out loud before," he adds. When I go quiet, coming to terms with what this all means, and being so caught by surprise, Rian gets nervous and impatient. "Say something, Maeve!"

"Oh, well, ah..." I don't seem to be able to combine enough words for a coherent thought. After all this time, I can't believe my brother kept this from me! Did he think I would care? That I wouldn't love him if he told me his secret? That couldn't be further from the truth. So, I try to figure out what to say to reassure him. There's only one thing I can think about. The poor thing. What if it's one-sided and he gets his heart broken? After all, Cormac is known for being a player, going through women like crazy. Does he go through men the same way?

"Does Cormac…do you think he loves you back?" I ask.

Rian shakes his head. "He's never said the words back, but I think maybe he does. And now all of this, taking a stupid bullet, could be his way of showing it."

"Wow. I really wish you would've told me before now," I respond.

Thinking back, this explains a lot about why Rian was so adamant about not leaving town. It wasn't about loyalty to the Irish or the cause, like our father. He didn't love the violence. Rian didn't want to leave the man he loved. Something like that, well, how can I argue with that when it's so sweet and romantic?

Squeezing Rian's knee to try and reassure him, I say, "I bet Cormac will be fine. He wouldn't have agreed to it if he thought it would kill him. He would run. He's selfish that way, and not stupid…"

"Maybe. Maybe not. Still, it's too dangerous!"

"Well, there's nothing the two of us can do about his decision right now," I remark. "How about we pray for him?"

"Pray? Seriously? Like that will do any fucking good!" he scoffs. Rian has always been skeptical of religion, and I can understand that better now. Why would he want any part of something that condemns him simply for who he loves?

"Praying is doing something when there is nothing else to do. It always makes me feel better, more at peace, if nothing else," I point out. Closing my eyes and bowing my head with my hand on Rian's knee, I pray aloud. "Lord, please watch over Cormac and keep him safe tonight and every other day. Help him be the best leader he can be. Please also keep the bikers safe and out of harm's way. Let all the men find forgiveness in their hearts to replace their anger and need for revenge. In your name we pray, amen."

"Thanks," Rian says when I open my eyes again. "I'm sorry I didn't tell you before. I just, I wasn't sure what you would think. I know dad would've hated it and probably killed me himself if he had known."

"Good thing he's not here, isn't it?" I reply. "Like he was perfect? You're a better man than our father, even if you do things I don't approve of – like starting a war with the MC."

"Yeah. That was pretty stupid. I should've tried to get Cormac to talk to them first. Apparently, the Knights were going to get out of the heroin business anyway, which was Cormac's whole issue."

"At least no one died," I tell him. "I'll keep praying for the injured biker to get better. If he doesn't live…"

"Then Cormac may have to take more than one bullet?" Rian finishes.

"Yeah. He could," I admit to him.

"Then I'll pray for the biker too," he says with a small smile.

"Good."

Getting to my feet, I walk around the small space to stretch my legs before sitting back down on the edge of the bed. "So, you said it was Wirth who worked out the deal with Cormac?"

"I think that's his name – big guy with broad shoulders and dark hair who answered your door and put the zip ties on me?"

"Yeah, that's him."

"His friends said he's got a huge set of balls to go into the pub alone," Rian adds.

"Hmm," I mutter. "He's a good man."

"They also mentioned he did it for a woman…"

"Oh yeah?" I try not to sound pleased by that and fail.

"Do you actually like him, or were you just playing him for information too?" Rian asks.

"I think I really liked him. He was better to me than I deserved," I say, thinking about Hunt's rage and how I could see in his eyes that he wanted to physically hurt me, possibly kill me for betraying the MC.

Wirth would never do that, though. I shouldn't have been so quick to think he had fooled me into thinking he was a good guy only to betray me.

My trust issues with men, thanks in large part to my father, know no bounds. And for that, I'm certain I owe Wirth an apology, especially after he figured out a way to keep my brother safe.

## CHAPTER TWENTY-THREE

*Wirth*

When we arrive at the pier, the only car in the lot is the black Jeep I remember from the Irish bar. We don't see anyone immediately, so we walk around the pier shop, which is locked up tight, and cut through the dock to the pier. We spot the ginger and two of his fair-haired buddies standing way down at the end. It takes us several minutes to walk all the way out to them. On the way, I watch Malcolm screw a silencer onto the 9 mm he has in a shoulder harness under his cut.

Malcolm waves everyone back as we get within earshot of the Irish, only keeping me close to him. Cormac looks between the two of us, giving me a nod before his gaze settles on Malcolm. "You're the president of the Dirty Aces," he states rather than asks.

Malcolm points at his patches and nods. "That's me. Wirth says you've already agreed to terms, but I want to hear you repeat them. Let's make sure we're all on the same page here."

"We had bad blood with the Knight's old president," Cormac sighs.

"Especially our former boss. They hated each other with a rare passion. Times have changed, and we need to change with them. Your man, Wirth, says that the Knights have patched over and are getting out of the heroin business."

"That's true," Malcolm agrees.

"Then we don't have any grievance with each other. There have been some mistakes made, but if we can put those behind us…" Cormac begins.

"We have one outstanding grievance," Malcolm corrects him.

With a sigh, Cormac replies, "But once that's settled, we'll be straight?"

"We'll be straight," Malcolm confirms as he holds out his hand for a shake.

Cormac accepts the handshake, then asks, "Where do we do this?"

"Right here will be fine," Malcolm says.

"All right," Cormac agrees with another heavy sigh. "Listen up boys. Part of the deal is that the Aces have to put a bullet in one of us. I volunteered."

The two fair-haired men standing behind Cormac had been silent up until now, but they both step forward to move in front of him before Cormac can wave them off. "This has to happen," he demands as he motions for them to step back. "This was ultimately my mistake, and I have to take responsibility for it. Once it's done, deal with my wound, and then go collect Rian. He'll be in charge now. You understand?"

The two men nod, both of them looking as if they are fighting back tears as Malcolm draws his pistol. He doesn't give Cormac a chance for any final words or monologuing. He simply pulls the trigger once, causing Cormac to jerk backwards against the pier railing.

"FUCK!" Cormac grunts as his hand raises to his shoulder. He looks at Malcolm in surprise, and with a hint of terror in his eyes.

"We're good." Malcolm says as he slides the pistol back. "Have your boys take you over to the hospital to get that cleaned. Should be through and through, just like your guys shot me. Get yourself patched up; we'll send Rian and his sister to you."

"Thank you..." Cormac gasps as his men help him straighten up and begin walking him down the pier.

"Next time you get a wild hair up your ass, you call me first," Malcolm threatens as Cormac is led away. "Don't make us go through all this again!"

Cormac's only reply is a pained grunt as he's helped to the Jeep.

"Nash, call Dev or Silas and tell them to let everyone go," Malcolm orders. "Tell them where Cormac will be so they can go check on him, or have the prospect drive them wherever they want to go."

Nash raises an eyebrow as he comes over and pulls out his phone. "Even if they want to go to Wirth's house?" he tries to joke.

"Wherever they want to go," Malcolm confirms. "Whatever's going on with you and that girl, Wirth, you need to sort it out. Don't bring any more fucking trouble to our table over this woman, you understand?"

"She isn't going to want to see me anymore," I protest.

Malcolm and Nash both snort at me, causing an angry red flush to rise to my cheeks. "She'll be crawling up his pole by tomorrow," Malcolm quips to Nash.

"Tonight," Nash corrects him with a grin.

I stomp off down the pier, irrationally irritated with both of my brothers after their ribbing.

## CHAPTER TWENTY-FOUR

*Maeve*

"You're both free to go," the guy with long brown hair says when he comes into the bedroom. Malcolm, I think his name is. He pulls out a big knife from the holster on his belt and cuts off Rian's zip ties.

"How is he? How's Cormac?" he jumps up and asks as soon as he's free.

"He's going to be fine. Just grazed his shoulder like the bullet grazed mine. It burns like a son of a bitch but will be fine in a few days," Malcolm replies. "The prospect can give you both a ride to the hospital if you want. Cormac's going to say he got hit while shooting at a range in the backyard with some drunk friends to try and keep the police away."

"Let's go," Rian says to me as he rushes out of the room.

"Thanks for not killing him," I tell Malcolm.

"No problem," he says. "I'm getting soft in my old age. Having a kid and an old lady doesn't help. They need me, so I can't be trigger happy anymore."

"Yeah," I agree as I follow him out of the house where Rian is already climbing into an SUV with the former Knights' prospect, Freddie.

I quickly look around, hoping to find Wirth to apologize to him and see where we stand.

"He's not here," Malcolm says, having figured out what I'm doing. "He said he had some work to do back at the shop."

"My car," I mutter, because I know that's what he's probably working on despite everything that happened.

"You nearly got him and the rest of us killed," Malcolm reminds me. "Better figure out a way to make that shit up to him."

"I will," I agree. "Where's his shop at?" I ask, and he rattles off the address.

"It's only a few blocks from the pool hall."

"Okay, thank you," I tell him just as Rian rolls down the passenger window of the running SUV and yells, "Hurry up, Maeve!"

Since I know I would be frantic to see the man I love after he was shot, I wave goodbye to the Aces and jog over to climb in the back.

"Sorry," I say. "Let's go see how Cormac is doing."

∽

Wirth

I've got the rear axle out of Maeve's car, and I'm working on getting the new one installed, when I spot her standing outside the open garage door, shifting her weight nervously from one foot to the other.

"You can come in," I finally call to her.

"You don't have to do this right now," Maeve says when she comes into the shop, her heels clicking on the concrete.

"It needs doing. Now is as good a time than any," I reply.

"Why didn't you come by the house earlier when they let us go?"

"Wasn't sure if you would want to see me," I admit.

"See you? I want to do more than see you," she says. "I owe you so much…"

"You don't owe me shit. I've told you that from the beginning," I snap at her. I don't want another second of this…whatever this is with her, to be about trading favors.

"And that makes me want you even more," Maeve says, coming up and wrapping her arms around my neck.

As she moves closer, I notice a dark tinting around her throat, bruising in the shape of big ass hands. "What the fuck happened? Did one of the guys hurt you?"

"It's nothing," she says, brushing it off. "Hunt was angry with me and he had every right to be upset. Can you really blame him? I deserved it."

"And he'll deserve my fists slamming into his goddamn face," I threaten.

"No, Wirth. Please just let it go. Please?" she begs and it makes it nearly impossible for me to refuse her anything, even this. At least for now… "I've put you in enough danger as it is. And I'm so sorry, about everything. I can't tell you how much it means that you got everything settled between the Irish and the MC. I don't think I've ever met a man like you before. It's no excuse, but my history with men has left me very…jaded."

"Yeah, I noticed," I mutter.

"The first man I was ever with bought my virginity from my father," she says. It's one of the most vile, disgusting things I've ever heard. In fact, I can't even begin to understand the type of person who could do that.

"I'm sorry that happened to you, doll," I tell her, and she shakes her head.

"I couldn't believe that not only did the person I trusted more than anyone do that to me, but that a stranger could also be so callous. It felt like…like I didn't have anyone on my side at the time and that I probably never would. But I was wrong," Maeve says. "I'm not telling you what happened in my past to try and gain your pity. It's just an explanation for why I wouldn't let myself trust that you were a good man."

"I don't know if I'm a good man or not," I admit to her. "I just want to make you happy and keep you safe."

"And that's all I need," she agrees, pressing her lips to mine. Pulling away, she adds with a smile, "Amazing sex doesn't hurt either."

"No, it does not," I agree. "But that's only the beginning," I promise her.

# EPILOGUE

*Wirth*

*A week later...*

"Wake the fuck up! It's homecoming day, motherfucker!" Devlin exclaims as all five of us barge into the bedroom at Joanna's house. Last night she finally made the call, telling Nash that Fiasco had been fever free for four days, had finished up the antibiotics, and that his wounds were healing great.

"Go to hell," Fiasco says before he covers his head with a pillow.

"Fine, we will, but we're taking you with us," Malcolm declares as he rips the pillow away from the grumpy man and Silas pulls the bedsheets off of him. Thankfully, he's wearing a pair of boxer briefs or the joke would've been on us.

"Go easy on him!" Joanna warns from the doorway. "He's still healing from two gunshots."

"I'll take his shit to the car," Nash says as he throws Fiasco's clothes and all into his bag. On the way out of the bedroom, he pulls a thick envelope from his back pocket and hands it to his sister. Not that she knows that yet. Maybe he's never going to tell her.

"You've already paid me plenty," Joanna says.

"Take it," Nash insists. "For the time you missed from work and meds you had to steal. Least we can do."

The rest of us know that it's more than that – Lucy told Nash that Joanna's bank account was low and that her mortgage was two months late.

"Thank you," the woman finally agrees before she takes the envelope.

"No, thank you," Nash replies before he walks out of the room with Fiasco's things.

"If you all have any other medical emergencies, you know where to find me," Joanna says, which is nice of her to offer.

"You're a goddamn saint," Malcolm says, kissing her cheek on the way out with Silas and Devlin behind him.

"What the fuck am I supposed to wear home?" Fiasco asks when he looks around and all his clothes are gone.

"Hold on," Joanna says before she goes to the closet, Fiasco watching her just as closely as before whenever I visited. Pulling out a blue robe, she takes it over to Fiasco and helps him put his arms in it.

"Nice look, man," I tease him. "Now let's go," I say when I start for the door, in a hurry to get back to my woman, who is at the pool hall with the rest of the old ladies, preparing a welcome back bash for Fiasco.

"At least you're all covered up now," Joanna says to Fiasco. Glancing over my shoulder, I see her pulling the two sides of the robe together and then Fiasco's hands shoot out, cradling her face in his hands to kiss her.

I should've kept walking, but I'm too stunned to look away.

It's a surprisingly gentle, sweet kiss, one that goes on and on until there's definite moaning coming from both of them.

Holy shit.

"Fiasco!" I yell to get his attention before the other guys come back.

Both of them jump like they didn't realize they had an audience to their moment. Joanna's face is flushed as she takes a step back while Fiasco doesn't seem inclined to leave.

"Come on, buddy," I say when I go over to grab his elbow and urge him along. "You're still surviving two gunshot wounds. No reason to make Nash add a third or a fourth."

"It would be worth it," Fiasco says.

"What?" Joanna asks. "Why would Nash care…"

"Ah, see ya, Joanna. Thanks again for everything!" I call back before hurrying Fiasco out of the house. I'd rather not start answering questions today and avoid whatever fallout might come from Fiasco, Joanna, and Nash all airing out their laundry.

Although, I get the feeling that it's only a matter of time before that shit goes down and takes a piece of the Dirty Aces MC with it.

*The End for Now…*

COMING SOON

Thank you so much for reading Wirth!

Fiasco's story is up next! Order your copy now!

# ABOUT THE AUTHORS

*New York Times* bestselling author Lane Hart and husband D.B. West were both born and raised in North Carolina. They still live in the south with their two daughters and enjoy spending the summers on the beach and watching football in the fall.

Connect with D.B.:
Twitter: https://twitter.com/AuthorDBWest
Facebook: https://www.facebook.com/authordbwest/
Website: http://www.dbwestbooks.com
Email: dbwestauthor@outlook.com

Connect with Lane:
Twitter: https://twitter.com/WritingfromHart
Facebook: http://www.facebook.com/lanehartbooks
Instagram: https://www.instagram.com/authorlanehart/
Website: http://www.lanehartbooks.com
Email: lane.hart@hotmail.com

Join Lane's Facebook group to read books before they're released, help choose covers, character names, and titles of books! https://www.facebook.com/groups/bookboyfriendswanted/

**Find all of Lane's books on her Amazon author page!**

**Sign up for Lane and DB's newsletter to get updates on new releases and freebies!**

Printed in Great Britain
by Amazon